A KATE SHUGAK MYSTERY

A Fatal Thaw

Dana Stabenow

D0057759

BERKLEY PRIME CRIME, NEW YORK

A FATAL THAW

A Berkley Prime Crime Book / published by arrangement with the author

PRINTING HISTORY
Berkley edition / January 1993
Berkley Prime Crime edition / March 1994

The Penguin Putnam Inc. World Wide Web site address is http://www.penguinputnam.com

ISBN: 0-425-13577-2

Berkley Prime Crime Books are published by The Berkley Publishing Group, a division of Penguin Putnam Inc., 375 Hudson Street, New York, New York 10014. The name BERKLEY PRIME CRIME and the BERKLEY PRIME CRIME design are trademarks belonging to Penguin Putnam Inc.

PRINTED IN THE UNITED STATES OF AMERICA

19 18 17 16 15 14 13 12 11

for
the Four Major Food Groups
& Literary Society
you know who you are
and you know why

A Fatal
Thaw

one

IT WAS SIX A.M. on the first day of spring, and although
sunrise was still half an hour away, when Kate opened her
eyes the loft of the cabin was filled with the cool, silvery
promise of dawn. She sat up, stretched and yawned, and
flung back the covers.

Pulling sweats on over her long underwear, she
shimmied down the ladder from the loft into the cabin's
single, square room. "Hey, girl." Mutt stood pressed up
against the door, ears cocked, iron-gray ruff standing
straight up around her face, yellow eyes wide and fixed
imploringly on Kate. "In a minute. Hang on."

Going to the stove, Kate opened the fire door and
stoked the fire from the wood bin next to it. The coals
from the night before were still hot and it only took a
moment for the wood to catch. She went to the sink and
pumped up some water to replace what had evaporated out
of the gallon-sized kettle overnight. Straining a little, she
set it back on top of the stove. "Okay, girl," she said. Mutt
danced with impatience as Kate stamped her bare feet into
boots, and then, as Kate got down the choke chain and
leash, her tail went between her legs and she whined, a
soft, piteous sound.

"Forget it," Kate said severely. The scar on her throat,
a whitish, flattened rope of twisted tissue stretching from
ear to ear, pulled at her vocal chords in protest at this early-
morning use, and her voice rasped like a rusty file over

her next words. "I saw that old he-wolf hanging around yesterday. I know you're looking to get that itch of yours scratched but the last thing we need underfoot is a litter of pups." Mutt flattened her ears and furiously wagged an ingratiating tail. "Don't try that sweet talk on me. I remember what happened last time even if you don't."

Mutt heard the inflexible note in Kate's voice. Her tail stilled, her muzzle drooped and she gave a deep sigh. Conveying the impression that she had been beaten into it, she submitted meekly to the leash, and slunk through the door and around the woodpile.

Kate let the leash run all the way out to give her some privacy and waited. She breathed in deeply of the cool morning air, smelling of pine resin and wood smoke. The big, round, flat-faced thermometer fixed to the wall of the cabin read twelve degrees, and it was only six-thirty. Yes, spring was finally here, at last.

She felt a single, experimental tug on the leash. One large yellow eye peered over the woodpile. "Not a chance," Kate told her, and took her turn in the outhouse without loosing her grip on the leash.

The killer woke a few moments later, twenty-five miles to the east, and rose at once, whistling. He washed his face and brushed his teeth, slowly methodically, a deliberate ceremony to his movements. Shaving was almost a ritual, and he was very careful not to nick himself with the blade. The new clothes—Levis, a Pendleton shirt, socks, T-shirt, shorts, bought the day before in Niniltna—had been pain stakingly laid out on his bed in the order that he would put them on.

The clerk at Niniltna General Store hadn't recognized him yesterday, in spite of his shopping there all winter long. He wiped the last of the shaving cream from his face and smiled at himself in the mirror.

Kate ate the last of last week's bread as toast dunked in her morning coffee. She mixed up a batch of dough and turned

it into a buttered bowl. Covering it with a damp kitchen towel she sat it next to the wood stove to rise. Puttering around the cabin, she changed the sheets on the bed in the loft and the towels next to the sink, scoured out the sink, cleaned the top of the stove, took the rag rugs outside to shake, and swept the hardwood floor. Pumping up enough water to fill the washtub, she added soap and clothes and left it on the wood stove to heat through. She cleaned the chimneys and trimmed the wicks of all the propane lamps. It was her usual Monday morning routine and she performed it on automatic. It was good to have a routine. It got things done, and it kept her too busy to think too much on how isolated she was. In the middle of 20 million square acres of national park in Alaska, where her closest neighbors were the grizzly sow across the river just waking up after a long winter's nap and the he-wolf sniffing hopefully around her horny husky, if she let herself she could get to feeling pretty lonely. Kate never gave herself enough time to feel lonely.

Chores complete, she sat down at the table next to the oil cookstove and pulled the one-pound Darigold butter can toward her. Dumping it out, she began to separate bills and stack coins. When she was through she had the grand sum of $296.61.

"Well," she told Mutt, "better than at breakup last year. At least we're going into this spring solvent."

Mutt wagged her tail in halfhearted agreement.

The Winchester Model 70 30.06 was new, purchased just the day before, from the same general store in Niniltna that had sold him his new clothes, from the same incurious clerk. The bullets were new as well, a dozen cardboard boxes of shiny new cartridges, 180-grain hunting ammunition, Winchester (he was loyal to the brand) Super X Silvertips, twenty rounds to the box. He succumbed to temptation and opened one of the boxes, pulling out a round. Even in that early light the brass gleamed, the

copper glowed and the silver shone. He'd never seen anything so beautiful.

He set up a row of empty cans and bottles on a sawhorse placed across the road leading to the lane outside his cabin. From the crossbar he hung a paper target, a series of concentric circles.

He paced off 150 yards down the old, straight railroad bed that served as the Park's main, and only, road. The hard-packed snow of winter was beginning to melt and break up beneath his feet. He squatted and set the boxes of ammunition to one side. Taking the rifle in both hands, he held it to his face for a moment, inhaling the fragrance of the oiled walnut stock, running an adoring fingertip down the gleaming black barrel. The bolt worked smoothly, the craftsmanship of the piece evident in each planed and polished surface, all the machined parts working together to form a perfect whole.

He pulled the stock firmly into his shoulder and sighted down the barrel. The tiny metal bead at the end of the barrel seemed at once so close and so far away. The metal was so new it glistened in the early morning light. He frowned, and felt around in his pockets for a match. Striking it, he held it so the smoke rising from it blackened the bead.

He looked at the factory sights and shook his head with an indulgent smile. From another pocket he produced a Williams Foolproof peephole sight and mounted it next to the receiver. He loaded the rifle, five in the magazine, one in the chamber, and stood. He pulled the stock in tight and sighted through the aperture, noting that in spite of the overwhelming whiteness of the surrounding snow pack the dulled black bead at the end of the barrel stood out clearly, with no distracting reflection of light. He squeezed off six shots, enjoying the cracking sound of the reports, the solid thump of the butt into his shoulder, the smooth action of the bolt between rounds. When the chamber was empty, he walked back up the road and inspected the target. Most of his shots were grouped above

and to the left of the bull's-eye. He adjusted the peephole sight with a small screwdriver, reloaded, and repeated the process. The third time he shot at the bottles and cans.

It took him less than an hour. When he was done, he had a killing machine that would reduce the three hundred yards between target and shooter to point-blank range. "A dead shot," he said, and smiled. And his wife had accused him of having no sense of humor.

He reloaded, and was careful to switch on the safety afterward. He didn't want to hurt himself.

"No, I said, and no, I meant," Kate told the door. Mutt whined mournfully behind it. "Besides, take it from me, men are nothing but trouble."

She pulled hard on the knob to see that the door had, in fact, truly latched, and turned to walk to the garage. Its double doors swung open easily, now that a winter's worth of ice and snow packed around the sill had melted down.

The building was an unheated shell made of three-by-six sheets of plywood on a frame of two-by-fours. A row of windows, encrusted with a year's worth of grime and mosquitoes, shed little light on the interior. The inside was lined with long strips of fuzzy pink fiberglass insulation between the studs, and shelves bolted to the studs, floor to ceiling and wall to wall. The floor was made of rough, unplaned planks. There was a red metal tool chest as tall as Kate mounted on wheels standing in one corner, a table saw in another and a counter with a line of power tools hanging from a pegboard nailed up above it. Unfinished and utilitarian, the garage was neat, reasonably clean and arranged so that everything in it was immediately ready to hand. Kate swept the tools with a stern eye and was satisfied that none of them had rehung themselves carelessly in her absence.

She went around the snow machine parked in front to the pickup truck behind it. It was a small diesel, an Isuzu Trooper, with a homemade toolbox mounted in the bed

behind the cab. She popped the hood. She'd disconnected
but not removed the battery when the first big snow fell
the previous autumn. Now she took it out and set it on
the counter. She left the garage and went to the generator
shed. The Onan 3.5KW had been new last fall, but it was
also diesel and balked at an easy start as a matter of prin-
cipal. She bled off some air from the compression-release
valve and, grunting, gave the hand crank a few more turns.
The engine caught, and she winced away from the resulting roar. She shut the door on it and returned to the garage.
A single, 150-watt light bulb she had forgotten to turn off
in February lit up the dim interior. She hooked the truck
battery up to the trickle charger and left it.

As an afterthought she went around to the back of the
cabin and climbed the wooden ladder to the rack that held
the diesel fuel tanks, a dozen fifty-five gallon Chevron
drums mounted on their sides, connected with lengths of
insulated copper tubing to each other, the cabin and the
generator shack. Pulling the dipstick from its rack next
to the ladder, she tested each barrel. The diesel was used
only to run the truck, the cabin's oil stove and the generator
to run the power tools in the garage, so the barrels were
all about a quarter to a third full. It was enough to see
her through to late May or early June, when the road
opened up and the tanker from Ahtna could get through.
"Close enough for government work," she said out loud,
and wiped the dipstick and capped the last barrel.

She went back into the house and reappeared with
a bucket of soapy water, a sponge and a squeegee
and began to wash the windows on the garage. After
a while the sun grew warm enough to remove her
sweatshirt and work in shirtsleeves. "Bet we hit thirty-
five today," she said. She stopped and looked guiltily
at the cabin. Huge yellow eyes stared reproachfully out
at her from the window over the sink. "Get your paws
off the counter, dammit," Kate called, but her heart
wasn't in it. Something halfway between a whine and

a howl was the reply, and she sighed and put down the squeegee.

Mutt greeted her at the door with ecstatic yips and tried to weasel her way outside. Kate wound one hand in her ruff and with the other reached for the choke chain and leash. She led Mutt outside, slipped the choke chain around Mutt's cringing neck and fastened the leash to a length of wire stretched between two trees at the edge of the clearing. The leash was just long enough to let Mutt run up and down the length of the wire without tangling itself. Mutt immediately dropped to her belly and, without a trace of shame, groveled for freedom.

"Don't look like that," Kate told her. "You know it's for your own good."

The killer donned hat and jacket and gloves and shouldered the rifle. He took the little mirror from its nail on the wall and held it at arm's length to survey his appearance. He frowned and made a minute adjustment to the collar of his shirt. His brows puckered a little over the wrinkling effect of the rifle's strap on his new mackinaw. He smoothed the jacket down with one hand, readjusted the strap just a hair to the left, and was satisfied.

He looked around the cabin. It was spotless, the chipped white porcelain of the sink scrubbed clean, the stove top scoured and gleaming blackly, the floor swept, the bunk made up neatly beneath its olive-drab army blanket. He nodded his head, pleased. No one was ever going to be able to say he wasn't a good housekeeper.

His first stop was a mile down the road. He enjoyed the walk, the cool, calm air, the chittering of the squirrels. Once he paused and cocked his head, certain that he'd heard a golden-crowned sparrow trill out its trademark three descending notes, Spring Is Here. It didn't repeat itself, and he moved on.

When he came into the clearing of the next cabin down the road, he met his neighbor coming in from the outhouse.

He was greeted, if not with enthusiasm, then at least with civility. "Hey, hi there. Great first day of spring, isn't it? Want some coffee?"

He turned toward the cabin and the first bullet caught him in the back, severing his spinal cord and exploding out of his chest in a hole six inches across. The second bullet went in the back of his neck and ripped out the front of his throat, changing his last terrified scream into a bubbling gurgle of bewilderment.

The sun was high and warm in a clear, pastel sky, and the thermometer on the cabin wall read twenty-eight above. "Told you so," she said to Mutt. Setting the chisel with a few taps of the blunt side of the axe, she stood back, raised the axe over her head, and brought the blunt side down on the chisel. The round of pine had seasoned through the winter and split cleanly at the first blow, with a satisfying crack, into two almost even halves. "I'm giving a loose to my soul," she told Mutt. Mutt yawned and settled her chin on crossed forepaws. Her choke chain was pulled tight, her leash stretched as far as it would go between choke chain and wire, and the leash run as far as it could get from where Kate was chopping wood. She was not speaking to Kate, but she still had plenty to say, all of it eloquent. Properly chastened, Kate reversed the axe and used the blade to spilt each half into two chunks.

A jangle of chain and a flurry of hysterical barks interrupted the splitting of the second round. She looked up to see Mutt prancing frantically, in a manner wholly unsuited to her age and dignity, at the extreme end of the wire closest to the edge of the clearing. Every hair on her body strained against the leash. Kate followed her gaze and drew in a breath.

He was a timber wolf, ash gray in color, standing three and a half feet tall at the shoulder and weighing, Kate estimated, a hundred and sixty pounds. His eyes were large, brown and probably usually filled with intelligence.

Today they were bright with something else, and they were fastened on the half-wolf, half-husky tethered to the wire next to Kate's cabin. He shook his coat into amorous order, adjusted the curl of his tail and stalked forward.

He was, all in all, a very handsome fellow indeed. Well, Mutt was no hag herself, and Kate understood the impetus behind and almost wavered beneath the onslaught of imploring yips and entreating howls from both lovers. She managed to pull herself together, though, and spoke in a stern voice. "Dammit, Mutt, I told you. We don't need any more puppies around here. The last bunch like to drove both of us into running away from home. We're lucky they turned out to be halfway trainable so Mandy could put them to work."

Mutt ignored the voice of reason, quivering, her ruff standing straight up, her tail curled coquettishly, her wide yellow eyes fixed on the wolf. He paused in his approach, glancing for the first time in Kate's direction, taking her in at a single glance and dismissing her as negligible. Kate wasn't quite sure she even registered on his peripheral vision as human and therefore a potential threat; his attention was clearly fixed elsewhere.

She moved over to the wire. Mutt danced around her eagerly, and Kate took one cautionary wind of the leash around her forearm, regarded it for a moment and took another. "Never underestimate the power of love," she muttered, and Mutt proved her point by almost jerking her arm out of its socket when Kate detached the leash from the wire. Mutt pulled avidly for the trees, Kate grimly for the cabin. Sweating, straining, and swearing all the way, the tug-of-war turned her hands and forearm dark red and numb to all feeling. Finally, Kate managed to get her shivering, whining roommate back inside and the cabin door safely closed and latched behind her. She subsided limply on the doorstep and mopped her overheated brow. "Besides," she told the eager scrabble of toenails against the other

side of the door, "if I can do without, so can you."

From the edge of the clearing the wolf howled, a long, lovelorn sound that rose to a frustrated crescendo. "Oh, shut up," Kate snapped, and returned to vent her spleen on the woodpile.

"Well, hey there, my first customer of the morning." The portly, cheerful man turned to face him across the counter. "The mail plane hasn't been in yet, so—"

The killer shot once. The expanding nose of the soft-tipped bullet shredded the back of the man's head and stuccoed the wall of wooden cubbyholes behind him in grayish white and dark red. The man's body stood, swaying for a moment, before slumping slowly and somehow gracefully to the floor.

There was a still, silent moment. The killer heard a quick, sharp intake of breath and wheeled to see the curtain that separated the post office from the rest of the house moving, as if someone had been holding it open and had just released it. He jerked it back, to reveal an empty living room, the door to it swinging wide. He went to the door and looked out, and saw her running down the long, narrow length of the airstrip, a pudgy little gray-haired woman in jeans and sweatshirt and stocking feet. He thought she screamed. A movement caught his eye and he looked beyond her. Two people on a snow machine broke out of the trees at the middle of the strip. The running woman yelled and waved her arms. The driver looked her way and turned the snow machine in her direction. The woman screamed and waved her arms more frantically.

The killer brought the 30.06 to his shoulder in one smooth motion and shot once. The driver slumped over the handlebars and the machine swerved abruptly. The passenger screamed and tried to shove the driver aside so she could grasp the handlebars, to no avail. She screamed again, and went on screaming, as the machine slewed and

swerved, back and forth, across the airstrip. Lining up the sight, the killer exhaled, held it and shot again. The screaming stopped abruptly. The snow machine, riderless, ran into the plowed snowbank at the side of the strip and flipped over.

He gave the Winchester a fond pat and looked around for the running woman. He found her all the way down at the end of the strip, stubby legs pumping tirelessly beneath the spur of adrenaline. Sighting carefully through the peephole, down the barrel and over the darkened bead that stood out so clearly against the hard-packed snow of the runway, he closed his fingers almost gently around the trigger, heard the shot and its echo immediately following, felt the kick of the butt against his shoulder, saw her stagger and fall. She lay still for a moment, before lifting herself up on her forearms and dragging herself into the trees. He shook his head, almost in admiration, and went after her.

He paused at the edge of the strip to look at the bodies of the two from the snow machine. He turned them faceup with one foot, careful not to let the blood dull the gloss of his new boots. One body no longer had a face, the other no chest. The killer straightened one's shirt, the other's legs, and followed the tracks into the trees.

A sharp crack echoed through the woods, and instinctively he threw himself down and rolled. He came up shooting, working the bolt and spacing his shots in an arc. He paused to reload, listening. There was complete silence, and then he saw the broken branch in one of his own footprints. He clucked at his over-reaction and recovered her trail. A few yards down it, he found the body.

He approached cautiously, rifle held in front of him, a round in the chamber and the safety off. Mukluks, bright pink bib overalls, a checked shirt. "Oh," he said, on a long note of discovery when at last he saw her face, and sank to his knees, beside her in the stained snow.

She was blonde and she was beautiful, even in death. The last time he'd seen her, that fair skin had been flushed, the full, red lips twisted away from her white, straight teeth in a sneer, the widely-spaced dark blue eyes narrowed in contempt. She had laughed at him.

He smiled down at her now, touched her cheek. It was cooling rapidly. He raised one lid to see if her eye was as blue as he remembered. It was. He admired the perfect fans her thick lashes made on her cheeks. His hand slid down her throat, shaped one breast, stroked her narrow waist, cupped between her thighs.

A small whisper, perhaps of wind, rustled through the grove. A sound, perhaps the whimper of a frightened squirrel, came from deeper in the stand of trees. It was enough to make him withdraw his hand.

He rose to his feet and threaded his way through the trees to the airstrip. Righting the overturned snow machine, he mounted it and thumbed the electric starter. It caught on the first try.

The pile of split wood was waist high when Kate heard the rapid whap-whap-whap of a helicopter's rotor. The sun was high in a still-cloudless sky, and her shirt was damp down her spine and beneath her arms. She sunk the axe into the tree stump that served as her chopping block and went inside to pump up a drink of water. She drained the glass, refilled it and brought it back outside, narrowly missing Mutt's nose in the door. She sat down on the front step, groaning a little from sore muscles. A rustle of underbrush called her attention to the edge of the clearing, where Mutt's would-be lover sat beneath a mountain hemlock.

For a change he was not looking yearningly at the cabin but in an inquiring fashion at the sky. She squinted up as the noise of the helicopter became louder, and jumped to her feet when it roared the last few feet to hover over her clearing.

"What the hell do you think you're doing?" she yelled, her voice a furious croak. "You can't land here!"

Mutt's lover decided it was a better day for discretion than valor and broke for the high country. As the Bell Jet Ranger with the distinctive blue-and-gold markings of the Alaska State Troopers lowered to the exact center of the clearing, Kate was forced back up against the door of the cabin. She held her breath, watching the ends of the rotors sweep dangerously close to the eaves of every building in the semicircle of her homestead.

The blades slowed their rotation but didn't stop. The engine powered down, and the door of the helicopter opened and a man in a state trooper's uniform emerged. Holding on to his hat, he crouched over the few running steps that brought him face to crotch with Kate.

She glared down at him. "What the hell do you think you're doing, Jim? You're lucky you didn't take the roof off everything I own!"

"Get inside!" he yelled, and suited word to deed by reaching around her to open the door and shove her inside, thudding up the steps and in behind her and pulling the door shut after him.

He was a tall man and a large one, and he filled up the cabin more than she liked. "What the hell do you think you're doing," she snapped, "pushing your way in here? What's going on?"

"You haven't heard?"

"Heard what?"

He strode over to her scanner and snapped it on, to be greeted by dead air. He shook his head and swore. "Dammit, I told them to broadcast a warning and keep broadcasting it until we catch the fucker."

"What fucker? What warning?" she said angrily. And then she saw his expression. In that instant her anger changed to apprehension. The words devoid of heat, she repeated. "Jim, what's going on?"

He turned and surveyed the room, Kate mystified, Mutt alert, both of them wary. "At least you're all right."

"Of course I'm all right." Kate's gaze sharpened. "Who isn't?"

His lips thinned. "Two people we know of, so far."

"Niniltna?" He nodded curtly, and she tensed. Next to her Mutt whined once, a keen, anxious sound. "What happened?" Kate said flatly.

He blew out a breath. "Near as we can figure, some guy's running around shooting at people with a 30.06."

Her mouth went dry. "Who?"

He shook his head. "We don't know yet."

"Who's been shot?"

A gleam of understanding crossed his face, but he shook his head again. "We don't that yet, either. He shot at the mail plane as it was coming in to land. George Perry saw some bodies lying at the end of the strip. Then a guy on a snow machine started shooting and he hit the throttle. He climbed to five thousand feet and circled long enough to put out an SOS. He saw the guy on the snow machine take off. That's about all we know, except . . ."

"Except?"

"Except that he's headed this way." The trooper saw Kate's reaction and nodded once for emphasis. "The mail plane called the tower in Tok, the tower called me, and I got in the air right away. I've been hitting every homestead on the way in."

Kate walked around him and got the shotgun down from the rack over the door. She broke it open to check that it was loaded. It was. She turned. "Okay. Now I know. You'd better get on with passing the word."

His expression relaxed, and he gave half a laugh and amazed her by swooping down for a swift, hard kiss. He laughed again at her expression and chucked her beneath the chin. "Probably the only chance I'll ever get, how could I resist?"

The shotgun was on its way up and if the helicopter hadn't been right in back of him she might even have fired off a round. He looked from her furious face to the shotgun and back, laughed again and actually had the gall to salute her. "If he gets here before I get him, he's wearing a black-and-red mackinaw and a brown billed cap with earflaps. He's driving a Polaris. Watch your ass, Shugak."

He ducked and ran to the helicopter. The engine pitch and blade rotation increased immediately. In five seconds he was in the air, in seven over the trees, and in ten out of sight.

"Go!" the farmer yelled at the two open-mouthed, petrified figures of his children. "Run, dammit!" He turned back to the killer and waved his arms. "Here! Over here, you lousy bastard! Come get me, I dare you!"

The killer looked at him without expression. The farmer, lying against his barn with a shattered leg and his life's blood oozing away, clutched frantically around him for something to throw. He found nothing but melting snow, and so he threw that, in handfuls that fell far short of their target in ineffective, disintegrating pieces. "Shit!" The killer watched him without moving. "Motherfucker!" the farmer yelled and flipped him the bird with both hands. "Joe! Mary! Run!"

The two children finally broke and ran, straight out across the frozen pond that fronted the farm buildings. The killer took half a step forward, swiveled and brought up the rifle. He frowned at the running figures through the sights. They were so small and they ran so fast. He squeezed off two shots. One hit, one missed. "No!" the farmer screamed, "no, no, no goddam you, no!" The killer shot a third time. The second figure fell hard on the grainy ice of the little lake and slid ten feet before coming to a stop.

The farmer, sobbing, crying, gasping for breath, was clawing his body to the edge of the lake when the killer

stepped up next to him. Their eyes met. The killer's face
was calm and still, the farmer's contorted with grief
and rage.

"Fuck you," the farmer hissed. "Do it."

Kate leaned the shotgun against the woodpile and picked
up the axe. After staring at it for a moment, she put the
axe back down and picked up the shotgun. She felt like
pacing, but pacing back and forth across the clearing with
a crazy person going around shooting at people seemed
like a bad idea. It might have been the safest thing to do,
but she couldn't bear the thought of cooping herself up in
the cabin. She turned to the woods. A frustrated whine and
an eager scratching at the inside of the door told her Mutt
had seen her. She paused. There was a rustle across the
clearing. The timber wolf was back. "Damn." In the state
she was in and with this embodiment of lupine perfection
hanging around, Mutt would be no use to her. Squaring her
shoulders, she walked across the clearing and up the path
that led to the road.

The miner vanished into the trees as the killer reloaded
the Winchester. The frantic, laboring sound of someone
crashing through thick woods and a winter's worth of
snow cover came clearly to him through the still air. He
threw in the bolt and cast a speculative glance toward
the sound. He stretched and yawned. The snow under
the trees was too darn deep to hassle with. The miner
would probably bleed to death anyway. Besides, he was
tired. His stomach growled. Hungry, too.

Kate was dozing when she heard it. At first it had
sounded like a single, distinct crash, like a large-scale
breaking of glass, but now there was no doubt about it.
It was a snow machine, and it was coming her way.

She'd walked from where the path that led to her homestead intersected the old railroad bed until she found a

long, straight stretch of the road. At the end of the straight stretch farthest from Niniltna, she searched out a squat, thickly branched spruce tree that was neither too close nor too far away from the edge of the road, stamped out a path and forced her way in between the branches. She squatted beneath it now with the shotgun resting across her knees. Peering out between the branches, she had a perfect view of half a mile of road, from where it curved to avoid Honker Pond to where she crouched.

The noise of the snow machine grew louder. The sky was clear and pale and innocent of helicopters or planes or any other kind of cavalry. "Damn you, Jim. Isn't that just like a cop, never around when you need him." When she looked back down the snow machine had rounded Honker Pond and was headed straight for her. There was no one else in sight.

She muttered a curse and clicked the safety off the shotgun. She rechecked the load, pulled the stock in against her shoulder, sighted carefully down the barrel, and waited.

The snow machine labored up the slight slope, until she could see his face, red from the force of the wind against it, lips pulled back from his teeth in a humorless grimace. It was a Polaris snow machine, all right, and the guy was wearing a red-and-black checked mackinaw and a brown-billed cap with earflaps. A chill shivered down her spine. She took her time lining up her shot. No matter what this yo-yo had done, she didn't want to kill him. She had enough on her conscience without another death, however justified.

He was almost upon her when the snow of the road exploded in front of his machine. Pieces of ice flew up and hit the windshield and his face. He yelled and jerked. The machine swerved. The handlebars ripped out of his hands and he fell, rolling awkwardly, slung rifle and all.

Kate plunged out between the branches of the spruce. One caught in her hair and almost yanked her off her feet.

She slipped and lost her grip on the shotgun. It smacked into the snow and slid several feet from her. Across the road, the killer staggered to his feet and unslung his rifle. She felt around and grasped a piece of deadwood and threw it at him as hard as she could. It caught him square across the face. He staggered a little. "Dog-gone it," he said. He recovered, and in one automatic action raised his rifle and sighted down at her.

Her hair still tangled in the spruce, the stock of the shotgun several feet away, Kate froze. She stared across the hard, packed roadbed into his calm, clear, quite mad eyes, and she knew she was staring at an escape from pain, a loss of laughter, the cessation of joy, all of them, straight in the face. She didn't move, couldn't.

He smiled at her. "Know anywhere around here somebody might get a bite to eat?"

There was a crash of tearing brush, and Kate was hit hard in the back of the knees. Her feet went out from under her, her hair ripped free of the branch and the world whirled around as she made a perfect backward somersault, landing on her chest with a thump that drove all the breath out of her.

Mutt's forepaws hit the killer square in the chest. He fell flat on his back with a hundred and forty pounds of proprietary rage on top of him. In a movement faster than Kate could follow Mutt clamped her teeth in the stock of the Winchester and shook it loose from his grip like a bear shaking off a mosquito. The rifle hit the ice six feet away and slid for twenty more. The killer lay where he was, dazed, his throat exposed, and Mutt lunged directly for it, her teeth closing in on either side.

Kate's breath returned with a rush. "Hold!" she shouted.

Mutt froze, her teeth indenting but not breaking the skin of his throat. "Hold, girl," Kate repeated, grasping at air, her voice a husky croak, "hold."

It took her two tries to climb to her feet. She stood where she was, trembling, eyes closed, gulping in great

breaths of air. Her chest hurt. Her scalp ached. Her lungs burned. Somewhere behind them the Polaris was still running. The engine rose in whiny protest, spluttered and died. Kate sucked in another deep breath and opened her eyes.

The killer lay where he had fallen. Mutt stood over him, teeth bared against his throat, a low, rumbling growl issuing unbroken from deep in her throat. In that moment she seemed all wolf. Kate recovered her shotgun and approached them warily. She reached his rifle, kicked it away. "All right, Mutt."

The dog lifted her head slightly, her teeth no longer touching the killer's throat, but that continuous, rumbling, paralyzing growl never stopped. "It's all right, girl," Kate said and reached out a steadying hand. Beneath it Mutt flinched once, and Kate tensed. "You done good, girl. Now let go. Mutt," she repeated, more sternly this time, "release." The growl missed a note, diminished, and died. Mutt looked up at Kate and gave her tail a single wag. Kate inhaled again and straightened. "Good girl." And then, more fervently, *"Good* girl."

The killer was conscious. He looked up at them calmly, all tension drained out of his body. He even smiled, a happy, bloody smile that reached all the way up into mischievous, twinkling eyes, one nearly swollen shut. He giggled. "You'll never guess what I've been doing." He giggled again. "I've been a bad boy." He licked the blood from his lips and appeared surprised. He raised one wondering hand, touched it to his mouth and looked at his stained fingers. "I'm bleeding," he said. His face puckered. "He should have sold me Board Walk. I told him. He should have sold it to me." He started to cry.

Kate took three faltering steps to the side of the road and was thoroughly and comprehensively sick, which was how Chopper Jim found her when he landed twenty yards down the road a few minutes later.

two

two

————————————
————————————

JACK Morgan sighed. "It's too bad everyone lived right on the road. McAniff didn't have to go out of his way any to find targets."

"No."

Jack tilted his chair back and crossed his booted feet on the top of his desk. A pile of paper six inches high tilted and almost slipped to the floor. He didn't seem to notice, and Bill Robinson, grumbling beneath his breath, bent forward to straighten it. It still amazed him how Jack, chief investigator for the Anchorage District Attorney's office, could find anything in that office in time for trial. Small, square and windowless to begin with, it was made even smaller by the overflow of file cabinets, crime scene drawings, evidence bags, three chalkboards covered on both sides with his boss's scrawling script and a stack of paper that started somewhere near the door and rolled across the room in drifts, like snow after a blizzard, to engulf Jack's desk. More paper in the form of maps were tacked to every square inch of the walls, with crime scene drawings taped over every square inch of the maps, all heavily marked with more notes in Jack's illegible scrawl. Jack leaned toward the black, broad strokes of a Marksalot for arrows, exclamation points and marginal balloons.

Even Bill had to admit that Jack's conviction rate proved that he could and did find what he needed when he needed it, though only Jack and maybe God alone

knew how. And it wasn't his office. He shook his head, not for the first time, and sat back in his chair to line up the corners on the neat stack of paper in his lap.

"Okay, Bill," Jack said, staring at the ceiling with his hands linked behind his head. "Run it down for me."

Bill turned a page, shuffled it to the bottom of the pile with meticulous precision, and cleared his throat. "His neighbor was the first to be hit. Name of Stephen Syms, 34. Lived in the Park year-round, fished in the summer, did what he could in the winter. His neighbors on the other side were the Getty sisters, Lottie and Lisa. They heard the shots at about ten A.M. and according to Lottie went over to take a look. By the time they got there, Stephen Syms was dead and McAniff gone. They looked for tracks and didn't find any, and there's only the one road, so they got out their snow machine and followed it into Niniltna."

Bill flipped a page. "Okay, scene shifts to Niniltna, post office next to the airstrip. Postmaster's name was Patrick Jorgensen, 63, moved to Niniltna in 1949, married, raised a family, been the postmaster there for the last twenty years. He was shot once at point-blank range. His wife, Becky Jorgensen, 64, saw it all from the next room and ran out the living room door and down the strip. McAniff must have heard something because he followed her out and shot at her, she thinks a couple of times." He looked up at Jack. "Her memory gets a little confused at this point, and who can blame her. He shot at her at least once, though, because she's got as neat a hole through her upper right arm as you ever saw. Swish, right through, didn't touch the bone or the artery." He shook his head.

"She was lucky."

"She wasn't the only one." He flipped to a third page. "About the time she got to the end of the strip—by the way, she couldn't tell me why she didn't duck into the trees on one side or the other. She just ran, flat out, trying to put as much distance between the rifle and her."

"Maybe between the mess it left of her husband of thirty-two years and her," Jack said gently.

"Maybe. It was a mess. So, she gets to the end of the strip and who should appear out of the trees but Lyle and Lucy Longstaff, both 24. He was a Park rat, hunted, fished, panned a little gold. She was a bank teller he met and married in Anchorage, on New Year's Day."

"This New Year?"

"Yeah."

"Jesus."

"Yeah. She quit her job in January and moved to his cabin down on Gold Creek. They'd come up to Niniltna to meet the mail plane." Bill was a square, stolid man with a square, stolid face without much expression. And yet, as Jack listened to him tick off the victims and their descriptions from his neatly typed list, Bill's counting-down acquired something of a dirge-like quality. In his careful enunciation of the names of the dead, in his use of their full names each time he said them, it was as if he were testifying to their very existence, to the space they had once occupied on the earth, in the only way he would permit himself. All cops know that emotional involvement in any case is fatal, to themselves and usually to the case. Many of them succeed in their work only by devising a kind of working separation of person and profession, sort of like church and state. Or they try to. The best succeed at least part of the time. And yet. And yet.

"So, McAniff shoots Lyle Longstaff and Lucy Longstaff; theirs are the two bodies George Perry, the mail plane pilot, saw lying at the end of the runway. McAniff went into the woods at the end of the runway after Becky Jorgensen, evidently shooting as he went, because here's where the fell hand of fate steps in.

"The Getty sisters made it in from Syms's cabin, and the first place they stop is the first place everybody stops coming into Niniltna."

"The post office."

"Right. They see Patrick Jorgensen laid out back of the counter and hear shooting down the runway. They split up and circle around the woods in back of the strip where they heard the shooting. McAniff lost Becky Jorgensen, then, and it looks like he lay down a screen of shots, trying to get her. Lottie Getty stumbled across Becky Jorgensen and they hightailed it out of there. It was just dumb bad luck Lisa Getty ran into one of McAniff's bullets." He paused. "She was a looker."

"I saw the pictures."

"Yeah. Thirty years old, looked like Marilyn Monroe, beauty spot, body and all. What a waste." Bill shook his head, and he turned to the next page. "So, Perry lines up for a final and all of a sudden finds the air over the strip filled with more bullets than a hot LZ and he was outa there."

"Understandable."

"He climbed out of range and circled for a while, looking down at the scene through binoculars. He saw McAniff head down the road to Ahtna, and he was the one who finally got a message through to Jim Chopin in Tok, who saddled up and headed out. Meanwhile, back at the massacre." He shuffled some more paper.

"John Weiss, thirty-seven, his wife Tina, thirty-five, and their two children, Mary, six, and Joseph, five, lived on a farm about ten miles out of Niniltna."

"Why didn't he shoot up the town when he went through?" Jack interjected.

"He didn't go through town, he went over the river and through the woods and picked up the road at Squaw Candy Creek."

Jack's feet came down with a thump. "Squaw Candy Creek. Bobby Clark lives on Squaw Candy Creek. Has anyone—"

"Black guy in a wheelchair, does the NOAA reporting from the Park?" Jack nodded, and Bill waved a reassuring hand. "He's okay. Chopper Jim checked on him." Bill gave a dour smile. "Jim says Clark was mad as hell that

McAniff *didn't* come his way, he would have shown the fucker how fancy *he* could shoot."

Jack sighed with relief. "That's our Bobby. Thank God."

"The Weisses lived in another house by the side of the road. Apparently Tina Weiss caught it first, in the outhouse. Near as we can figure, McAniff shot John Weiss once in the left thigh, after which Mary and Joseph ran out onto a little lake the farmhouse fronted on. McAniff shot them as they were about to make the trees on the other side. It was almost like he waited until they got that far before shooting."

"Gave them a sporting chance," Jack suggested acidly. "Who does this guy think he is, General Zaroff?"

"From the evidence it looks more like he was seeing just how good a shot he was." He met Jack's eyes. "Small targets, moving, that kind of thing."

Jack closed his eyes and said wearily, "Jesus Christ."

"John Weiss, who we think was conscious and saw all this, was trying to crawl out to them when McAniff walked over and shot him. One shot, right here." Bill demonstrated with a cocked finger to his left temple. "Point-blank range. Powder burns beneath the skin, casing next to the body. He just walked up, stared him straight in the eye, and shot him."

There was a brief pause as both men imagined the scene in their minds; the mother shot where she sat; the father allowed to live long enough to witness the cold and deliberate murder of his own children; the last, lone and by then probably welcome shot to the head. Jack's skin crawled, and he shook himself and got up to refill their cups. The coffee was hot and strong and burned going down, and it brought Jack back from that cold scene by the lake to the more prosaic surroundings of his crowded office.

"Next stop, the access road to the Nabesna Mine. It was just more dumb bad luck that had MacKay Devlin

turning onto the road to Niniltna when McAniff passed
by. He says he hung a right a little fast and skidded to a
stop on the old railroad bed right in front of McAniff's
snow machine. McAniff had the 30.06 out and up before
Devlin could blink his eyes, and Devlin says he just took
off running. He says McAniff shot at him five or six times,
which agrees with the number of casings we found at the
scene." Bill blew on his coffee and sipped at it. "Only
nicked him once, on the outside of the upper right arm.
Just like Becky Jorgensen. The McAniff specialty."

"Lucky for Mac."

"You know Devlin?" Jack nodded. "I think he was more
than just lucky."

"How so?"

"I figure McAniff must have been getting tired. At any
rate, he didn't pursue Devlin the way he did the others.
He got back on the snow machine and drove down the
road. And, as we all know now, about twelve miles later
he ran into Kate Shugak."

Not by a glint in the eye or a change of tone did Bill
betray knowledge of Jack's history with Kate, or of Kate's
previous employment on the Anchorage D.A. investigators' staff, but then he'd only been with them himself for
eighteen months. While highly unlikely, it was possible
the gossip had cooled off. Jack doubted it.

"Hers had been one of the homesteads Chopper Jim had
warned on the way in," Bill said. "She took her shotgun
out to the road, waited for him and bagged the bastard." He
drank coffee and observed, "Too bad she didn't kill him."

"She wouldn't."

"Seems a pity. Would have saved us a lot of time and
the taxpayers a lot of money."

"True."

"So." Bill began gathering the files into a pile. "What've
we got here? One, two, three, four, five, six, six, seven,
eight, nine, count 'em, nine murders in the first degree.
Jesus. And one, two attempted murders."

"Those two attempts include the try at Mac Devlin?" Bill looked up. "Of course. Why?"

Jack smiled, a small, wry smile but a smile nonetheless. "In the Park, shooting at Mac Devlin isn't quite the same thing as attempted murder."

"Then what is it?"

"I think it's more in the way of a team sport." Bill looked puzzled, and Jack said, "McAniff. Tell me about him."

Bill produced yet another manila file folder and opened it to the first page. "You know mass murderers virtually didn't exist until the sixties. Since then, there've been enough to begin building a profile."

"How fortunate for us."

"Yeah. Anyway, Roger McAniff fits the profile, so well it's scary. He's thirty-one, and M&Ms are usually in their twenties or thirties. He's five-six, which makes him a little shorter than average, and M&Ms usually are. He weighs in around one seventy-five, which makes him overweight, which also fits into the profile, but when you consider he's coming off an Alaskan bush winter, maybe that statistic doesn't mean very much in this case. He's got a mustache."

"Mass murderers got mustaches?" Jack said, smoothing down his own neatly trimmed mustache and beard.

"Most of them. Most of them are also usually white, usually male and usually likely to kill their victims in their victims' own homes."

"This guy is just typical as hell, isn't he?" Jack said, still stroking his beard.

"For a mass murderer," Bill agreed.

"When'd he move to Niniltna?"

"Last fall. He was working as a computer programmer for Alaska Petroleum."

"On the Slope or in town?"

"In town. There was a big rif—reduction in force—last September, and he got his pink slip then. About the same time his wife threw him out. According to the head of the

Niniltna Tribal Council—" Bill squinted at a page. "Billy Monk?"

"Billy Mike."

Bill made a careful note. "Right, Billy Mike, according to him, Talbot showed up in Niniltna around Halloween."

"Enter the boogeyman."

"In person."

"From what we can tell without the autopsy reports, he's a pretty good shot."

"Expert." Jack raised his eyebrows. "Literally. In the army,'80 to '83."

"See any action?"

Bill shook his head. "He was stationed in Panama. Not much going on there then."

"Didn't re-up?"

"Nope. Transferred to Fort Richardson in '83, took his out here."

"Army have anything to say about him one way or the other?"

"No, pretty much standard evaluations all the way across the board. However." Bill flipped to another page. "You'll like this. When the troopers searched his cabin, they found a computer printout of the names, phone numbers and home addresses of Parks Department employees, and another of Department of Public Safety employees, including fish hawks and the State Troopers' own Alert Team. Nine of 'em." He looked up. "Including Jim Chopin."

"Jesus Christ." The vexing problem of whether or not it had come time to shave forgotten, Jack dropped his hand from his beard and sat up. "Where'd he get those?"

Bill shrugged. "He worked with computers. Alaska Petroleum pumps half the oil out of Prudhoe Bay; theirs is one of the biggest and best. We've got their department head going through their hard drives now, trying to backtrack and see if he accessed state computers through

their system. Half the Department of Public Safety is
hanging over his shoulder."

"I'll just bet they are. Jesus," Jack repeated. "What the
hell was he going to do with those lists?"

"Who knows?"

"Has anybody asked him?"

"He's got a lawyer."

Jack grunted.

Bill straightened and stacked his papers into a neat pile.
"Doesn't really matter, anyway. With or without charging
him for attempted murder on MacKay Devlin, on conviction we should be able to put McAniff away for, oh, I'd
conservatively estimate, say, 299,999 years. Without benefit of parole."

Jack toasted Bill with his coffee mug. "I hear his lawyers are considering pleading insanity caused by eating
too much junk food and getting too little light in the winter."

Bill's mouth turned down. "I can see it now. We the
jury find the accused not guilty by reason of insanity,
caused from eating too many Twinkies and spending a
winter in the Alaskan bush. He'll probably be sentenced
to the Alaska Psychiatric Institute and be out on the streets
in two years."

"Nope. He'll still have to serve his time," Jack said. He
sat contemplating the prospect with patent satisfaction.
"According to the new 'guilty but mentally ill' provision
in the criminal code."

"That's right, I forgot. One of the smarter things the legislature has done in the last ten years."

"Maybe the only." The phone rang on Jack's desk and
he answered it. "Jack Morgan. Oh hi, Slim. What can I do
you for?" He listened. "What?" He listened some more.
"Are you sure?" An odd note in his voice made Bill look
up. Jack's eyes were narrowed and intent, looking at
something Bill couldn't see.

"Ballistics confirms? Did you—" Jack listened for a moment to the voice on the other end of the phone. He closed his eyes and shook his head. "Great. Thanks, Slim. I think."

He set the phone in its cradle with great care and looked across the desk. "That was Slim Bartlett."

"The coroner."

"Yeah. He's got some news about the autopsies on the Niniltna massacre victims."

"What?"

"First of all, Lucy Longstaff was pregnant."

Bill's lips tightened into a thin line. The wad of paper he held crumpled a little, and it took a conscious, visible effort to the relax the grip he had on it. He smoothed the sheets with exaggerated care. "So. Ten murders."

"No. It's still just nine." Jack paused. "Slim told me something else, too."

"What?"

"You're going to like this."

Bill Robinson was beginning to know Jack Morgan in this mood. He sat back and let him play it out. "The ice just went out at Nenana and I won?"

"Better." Bill waited. "Slim says that the bullet that killed Lisa Getty came from a different rifle than the one that killed the rest of the victims."

Bill straightened with a jerk. "What!"

"Yeah, I know."

"Shit!"

"Yeah," Jack Morgan said thoughtfully. "I know."

"Jim?"

The trooper shrugged. "We've collected all the evidence there was to collect, and your people have examined it." He nodded at the pile of file folders on Jack's desk. Bill Robinson leaned against one wall, watching the exchange. "Those are all the statements we took. You've read them. Lottie Getty and Becky Jorgensen

were together at the time Lisa Getty was shot. We tested Lottie's rifle and it came up clean. Becky was unarmed. George Perry never got on the ground. Hell, it was a Saturday morning. Usually pretty quiet in Niniltna on Saturday mornings, at least until the mail plane lands, and then everybody in town can hear it and they come out. Until then—" He spread his hands. "There's just no reason, or there wasn't, to suspect that anyone else was doing any shooting that day." He paused. "Is ballistics sure?"

"They're sure."

"Did you have them run another test?"

"And a third. They all come up the same. Lisa Getty was shot by a different rifle than the others."

"Damn."

"So," Jack said, studying his feet. "Where will you start?"

Heavy lids drooped over the trooper's eyes and Jack couldn't read the expression in them. "I'm afraid I can't start anywhere."

Jack stared at him in disbelief. "Why the hell not?"

Chopper Jim said evenly, "I was involved in a personal relationship with Lisa Getty recently."

Jack sat up. "How recently?"

"Recent enough to keep me out of this investigation now."

The trooper looked up, and the expression on his face was as close to defensive as Jack had ever seen Jim Chopin get. He was surprised it was even possible. He waited.

"It started New Year's Eve at Bernie's Roadhouse," Jim said at last. "It ended Valentine's Day at hers."

"Who broke it off?"

"She did."

Jack's eyebrows disappeared into his hairline. "Did you fight?"

"No." The word was brought out with unnecessary force, and Jack noticed it, and Jim noticed he noticed it,

and Jack noticed him noticing. Their eyes met and they both laughed at the same time.

"Gotta ask, Jim," Jack said, sobering.

"Yeah. I'm not—I don't—" For a moment the trooper was uncharacteristically at a loss for words. "Oh hell," he said, and gave a short, humorless laugh. "It's a little different," he said, his voice wry, "being on the other side."

"Yeah." Jack waited.

"It wasn't like we were in love or anything. It was just one of those things." If the legends were true, Chopper Jim went through "one of those things" on average about once a month. Jack sat back in his chair and regarded the man sitting across from him.

Even sitting down Chopper Jim looked every bit of his six-feet-ten-inch height and every one of his well-developed and superbly maintained two hundred and seventy pounds. On his feet, in the Alaska State Trooper's uniform, all blue and gold and badge and gun, Jim simply radiated authority and competence and strength and probity and rectitude; most if not all of the virtues and certainly none of the vices. If you squinted, he looked a little like John Wayne. If you didn't, he still did.

The appearance was something of a fraud as far as women were concerned. Beneath the flat brim of the hat, the calm, blue eyes could turn, without the slightest warning, deadly seductive. His jaw was firm and square and held up a quick, charming and totally untrustworthy smile. Chopper Jim always carried with him a musky whiff of having just rolled out of bed, and the seductive sense of being just barely able to wait until he got back in it, preferably accompanied. Jack had hoisted a few with the trooper, off duty and out of uniform, and he had to admit, not without a trace of envy, that not for nothing did they call Chopper Jim the Father of the Park. Kate herself was not entirely immune, he realized for the first time with a small shock, or she wouldn't have maintained such an air of implacable hostility around the trooper.

It remained to be seen how immune Lisa Getty had been.

Jim was speaking again. "We went at it hot and heavy for six, seven weeks. Then, on February 14th I flew into the Park and went to her house. It'd been a week since I'd seen her, and she was—well, never mind that. She let me in, and then she let me out again about five minutes later. She said," and Jim seemed to be trying to recall the exact words, "she said she liked me a lot, that it had been fun but it was time to move on, and she hoped there were no hard feelings. Then she opened the door and smiled at me." He paused. "She didn't even say she hoped we could still be friends. She did everything but help me outside with the toe of her boot." He shook his head. "I've never been given the bum's rush before. At least not like that."

"Another new experience for you," Jack couldn't resist saying.

Again, Chopper Jim surprised him. He gave Jack a crooked smile. "Sure as hell was. Sure doesn't happen to me a whole hell of a lot."

Jack thought about it. "She say why?"

The trooper shook his head.

"You didn't ask?"

The trooper shook his head more definitely this time. "There was no point. She was a very . . ." he cast about him for exactly the right words, and settled somewhat lamely on " . . . independent person. When she did something, she had her own reasons for it, and she didn't believe in wasting time explaining to whoever couldn't keep up."

"Another guy, you figure?"

"That's the obvious, most likely reason, I know. But with Lisa . . ."

"What?"

The trooper shrugged. "Lisa Getty was a lot of things. 'Obvious' wasn't one of them. She was a complicated lady."

"Just because she dumped you?"

For the third time Jim Chopin surprised Jack Morgan. He gave the question a detached sort of consideration. When it came, his answer was without emotion, given, indeed, with the dispassion of the trained investigator. He shook his head, back and forth once, decisively. "No. We were about as close physically as you can get, but . . ."

"But what?"

"But what." Jim studied his hat as if the answer were written under the brim. "She had this ability, this talent."

Jack raised his eyebrows a little over that. "Talent for what?"

"I don't know exactly what to call it. A talent for concentration, I guess. Maybe, compartmentalization?"

"Whoa."

"I told you, I don't know exactly what to call it. All I know is she had the ability to shut down the rest of her life while she was concentrating on one specific part." Chopper Jim fidgeted a little. Jack had never seen him fidget before, and he had to admit to himself that he enjoyed it. "When we were together, she concentrated on me, on us, on what we were doing. It was pretty . . ."

"Intense?" Jack suggested with a straight face.

Fidget, maybe, but nobody'd been able to embarrass Chopper Jim since the age of six. "I guess that's as good a word as any. It was only after it was over that I realized that, however intense it had been, I never did get to know her all that well."

"Great."

"Yeah," Chopper Jim said. "I know. I don't know if I should have tried to know her better, or never started up with her at all."

"It'd make this job that much easier if you had tried to know her better," Jack observed somewhat sourly.

Chopper Jim shrugged and leaned back in his chair. Confidences concerning his personal life were clearly at an end.

"What're we going to do about this?"

Chopper Jim shrugged again.

"If you can't go in, who're we going to send? No one knows the Park better than you."

"Oh, I don't know." Chopper Jim was readjusting the crease in the crown of his hat with a delicate precision Bill admired. "I'm sure you'll find someone capable of doing the job." He made a minute alteration to the twin tassels at the end of the gold cord encircling the brim. "Better be careful. You know how they are in the Park about protecting one of their own."

Jack thought back to the previous December and couldn't suppress an inner shiver. "Yes. I know. So?"

The trooper set his hat on his head, tilting the brim so that it came down low over his eyes. He looked up, his expression somewhere between rueful and resigned. "So. Looks like Kate's all we got."

"Looks like." Jack made a pretense of straightening a pile of paper on his desk.

"When you going in? Tomorrow?"

"No." Jack thought. "I'll have the team go over the ground one more time and bag everything that doesn't actually move out of the way. And I think I might have ballistics run the bullets through CLIS." He raised a hand in the face of Bill's unspoken protest. "I know, I know, but with Kate Shugak you want to make sure."

"Make sure of what?" Bill asked.

"Make sure there's no way she can back out of it," the trooper said shrewdly.

Jack's thick black eyebrows twitched together but he didn't rise to the bait. "I know a guy, Gamble, on the FBI. He owes me. He'll get them through the data base and get me a printout on the rifling characteristics pronto. I should be able to go into the Park on," he leaned forward to flip through his desk calendar, "at the latest, Sunday."

"Want a lift?" Chopper Jim said.

Jack shook his head. "I'll fly in myself."

Kate. His spirits rose. He was going home, to Kate, when he hadn't thought he would see her again until his vacation in May. His heart actually skipped a beat, and he couldn't keep the smile from forming. He looked from Bill's curious and slightly disapproving expression to the trooper's knowing one and laughed out loud.

three

KATE was replacing the window Mutt had charged through to her rescue nine days before. The sky was clear and calm, the sun warm on her back, the temperature above freezing and the task simple and straightforward, occupying her hands while letting her mind wander. That was the problem.

"Yes," she said, "there is something about apprehending murderers in mid-massacre that tends to take the edge off of spring fever."

Saying it out loud didn't help as much as she had thought it might. Grunting, she lifted the window in its prefab aluminum frame and settled it into the wall of the cabin. Through the glass Mutt looked at her pleadingly. Kate fumbled in her pocket for screws and began to set them in, one at a time, concentrating with a kind of stubborn determination. The horror of the scene on the road dogged her heels like a shadow, always on the periphery of her consciousness. It tarnished the promise of the early spring days and poisoned her dreams.

Across the clearing there was a rustle of brush and she looked around to see Mutt's boyfriend springing to his feet and looking up in the sky to the west. Kate paused and cocked her head. A faint buzz sounded the approach of an airplane. The noise became louder and lower, and she whipped her head

around just in time to see a blue, black and silver
Cessna 172 roar over the clearing, the gear nearly skimming the tops of the trees. A full-throated
baritone made itself heard above the engine, belting
out a song about dames and how there was nothing
like them.

She started to smile. The Cessna came around for a
second pass and another verse. She was grinning as she
grabbed her parka and ran for the garage, an indignant
and frustrated Mutt yelping from the cabin. As she
rolled the snow machine outside, the Cessna roared
overhead for the third time and the chorus. The Super
Jag unaccountably started at first try. Kate hit the throttle
and roared out of the garage without stopping to close
the door behind her, past the mystified wolf crouching
beneath the hemlock tree and up the path to the road,
without a glance or a thought to spare for anything
but how fast she could make the twenty-five miles to
Niniltna.

He should have been on the ground long since, but when
Kate got to the airstrip he was still circling the field and
continuing to sing out of the Cessna's open window. As a
dozen friends and relatives were later delighted to inform
her, in the interim he had made a couple of low runs over
the town itself and one foray out to the Roadhouse, ser-
enading all who passed beneath his wings. The two tribal
policemen on duty that day gaped up at him from one end
of the runway, so struck by this spirited rendition of Rog-
ers and Hammerstein that they didn't bother to turn as Kate
came up behind them.

As soon as he saw the Jag emerge out onto the open
snow at the head of the strip the pilot banked and side-
slipped into a landing, rolling out to within ten feet of
her and swinging the tail around with a flourish before
killing the engine. He was out of the Cessna before
it stopped moving and strode past the tribal police

to swoop down on Kate. She was proud she didn't squeal.

"Jack?" Pete Kvasnikof cleared his throat. He shuffled his feet. "Jack?" He cleared his throat again. Finally he set his rifle butt down in the snow and reached his free hand to tap timidly at the big man's shoulder. "Uh, Jack?"

Jack pulled back from Kate and looked down at her flushed face with satisfaction. He growled once, low in his throat.

"Jesus, Jack," Pete said, hoping he wasn't blushing himself, "Kate oughta put you on a leash."

Jack turned, arm firm around Kate's shoulders, and appeared to see Pete for the first time. "Oh hi, Pete. Go ahead, search the plane."

"Gotta pat you down, too," Pete said awkwardly.

"Sure, sure, I know the drill." Jack stood, arms stretched out at shoulder height, one eye on Kate to make sure she didn't step out of reach.

"Okay," Pete said, stepping back. "You're clean."

Another man came panting up. "No booze in the plane, either."

"Who're you?"

"Jack Morgan, Tom Will. He's a new hire."

"Glad to meet you." Jack gave Tom's hand a brisk shake and as a continuation of the same movement turned to steer Kate toward the Super Jag. "See you later, boys."

The sound of the snow machine's engine starting drowned out Will's reply.

Kate barely had the door open when Mutt crashed out between them and tore into the woods.

"Mutt!" Kate yelled. "Come back here!"

Jack took her arm and pulled her inside. "Jack," Kate said, trying to twist free, "let me go. I've got to go get her. Jack! She's in heat, dammit."

"So am I." Jack kicked the door closed behind him. A second later Kate was flat on her back in the middle of the

floor, a trail of discarded clothing between her and the door and a large, warm man sprawled on top of her. With tender lips and gentle bites he traced the scar that twisted around her throat like knotted twine. She squirmed a little beneath the tickling sensation. "You shaved," she murmured, nuzzling him. "How come?" He bit her to get her attention and she forgot what she had been going to say next.

The afternoon and evening passed too quickly, in laughter and loving and a midnight raid on the kitchen. Jack woke before her the next morning and lay quietly, watching her. Asleep, her face held a kind of stubborn concentration that made him smile, and sigh. Her skin was smooth and gold. Her eyes, with just the hint of an epicanthic fold, when open were large and a light, clear brown and tilted upward toward her temples. Her hair fell straight and all one length to her waist, with no hint of wave or curl, as black as a shadow at midnight and as soft as silk.

Awake and in motion, she was short without being stocky, lithe without effort and beautiful without trying, at least in his eyes. He touched her, and she woke as she always did, at once and immediately aware of herself and her surroundings. She smiled at him, a wide, irresistible smile, and he leaned down into it and into a kiss that ended some time later less gently than it began but all the more satisfactorily for that.

She went back to sleep afterward. He rose and dressed and went downstairs to pump up water to wash and make coffee.

She woke up an hour later, feeling gratifyingly used in various places but not near as used up as she had been. She smelled coffee and smiled. Dressing quickly in jeans, sweatshirt and thick socks, she swung herself onto the ladder and slid down, letting the uprights slip between her feet and hands. She hopped the last few feet and turned with a cocky smile.

He was seated at the table, wearing businesslike horn-rimmed glasses and surrounded by a dozen bulging manila file folders. Her smile faded.

"Coffee's on," he said without looking up, "and I sliced some bread."

He had his work face on. Curious, she hesitated for a moment, but she could tell he wanted her to ask, so she turned and headed outside. There was no sign of Mutt. She called and waited, called again. Still no response, and Kate swore beneath her breath, used the outhouse and returned to the cabin.

She poured coffee, piled a saucer high with bread and carried both to the table. Jack gathered his files together in a bulky pile and shoved them to one side. He pulled off his glasses and rubbed his eyes, and thought how to put it for maximum effect. In the end, bluntness won out. "Roger McAniff didn't kill Lisa Getty."

Kate's hand stilled on the butter knife. She sat looking down at the slice of bread as if she'd never seen white flour, water and yeast mixed together before in her life. When she raised her head, Jack smiled inwardly. "What did you say?"

"Ballistics says the bullet that killed Lisa Getty came from a different rifle than the bullets that killed the other victims."

She looked at him steadily. "Different rifle."

"Yup."

"Different shooter?"

"Looks like."

She put down the butter knife, balancing it just so on the saucer. When she put down the bread he knew he had her. Not much got between Kate and food.

"Before you ask, we double-checked for errors. I even had Gamble run the printouts on the rifle through the CLIS data base. Same answer, three times."

"Gamble," she said. "The suit you brought in last year?"

"Uh-huh." He indicated the files that littered the top of

the table. "Want to take a look?"

"No." She picked up her bread, spread it with salmon-
berry jelly and took a big bite. The words muffled, she
added, "But I will."

After breakfast, she retired to the couch with the files
and read steadily through the afternoon. At about three
o'clock she put down the one she was reading and went
outside. She climbed the ladder to the cache and rooted
around. There were two small packages of caribou steaks
and a moose roast, all that was left of her winter meat
supply. She brought it all down. It was still freezing
at night, but the days were warm enough now that the
meat would soon spoil. "Mutt!" she called. "You horny
bitch, get your hot behind home! Now!" There was no
reply. She hadn't really expected one. There were legends
about timber wolves and their stamina. Kate didn't know
whether to laugh or swear. In the end, she did both. "Oh
hell. Enjoy it while you can, girl."

Inside, she chopped all three packages into stew meat.
Lighting the propane cooker, she put her biggest stew
pot over the flame and into it sliced a can of bacon
and the two largest onions she could find in the root
cellar in back of the barn. Mincing a couple of large
cloves of garlic, she stirred then into the bacon and
onions. The smell made her stomach growl. Adding
the meat and dried herbs she sautéd the mixture until
it was brown. She found some celery that wasn't too
withered and some carrots in excellent shape. She produced a couple of cans of stewed tomatoes and tossed
those in, too, filled one of the empties with water and
added it, thought it over and added two more. The
liquid in the pot barely covered the ingredients. She
cleaned the kitchen, waiting for the pot to boil, and
when it did added a couple of cups of macaroni, covered the pot and turned down the heat. She'd brought
another loaf of bread with her from the cache, and she
left that out on the counter, still wrapped in tin foil.

Jack, who had spent a peaceful afternoon reading his way through her collection of F. M. Busby, marked his spot in *The Long View* and sniffed appreciatively. "Can I help?"

"Nope."

He regarded her back with a speculative eye for a moment, decided against insisting, and reopened his book. Giving the counter a last wipe with the washcloth, she hung it over the pump and went back to the files. An hour later she finished reading the last file and sat, frowning at it. The stew was simmering, a cheerful, bubbling sound, and the aroma of garlic and onions and moose and caribou filled the house. Turning the cooker off, Kate set the pot out on the step to cool and called again for Mutt, in vain. It was still light out but she got a start on the evening by lighting the lamps, and the room was filled with a cozy, hissing glow.

Shelves lined every available inch of all the walls of the cabin except what backed up the two stoves. Most of the shelves were jammed with books, old and new, hard covered and paperback, all showing signs of being read and reread and read again. One of the shelves pulled out to form a rudimentary desk with stuffed cubbyholes directly behind it. Kate dragged a chair over from the table and rummaged around until she found paper and pen. She sat for a moment, thinking, and then bent over and began to write.

Eyeing her unresponsive back was unproductive and less fun than Rissa and Bran were having with UET. Jack went back to his book.

At six she brought the stew back in and reheated it. Jack dog-eared his book and went to set the table. At the first bite of stew he closed his eyes in momentary ecstasy. "Good," he said indistinctly. "Maybe your best."

They both had seconds and mopped up the juice with hunks of bread torn from the loaf.

"That was great," Jack said, leaning back with a satis-

fied sigh. "I don't know how long it's been since I had
moose stew. Too damn long. No, don't. I'll get it." He
smothered a burp and rose to clear the table. Kate went
back to the desk. Filling the dish pan alternately from
the gallon teapot sitting on the wood stove and the water
pump, he washed the dishes, put the remains of the stew
into a smaller pot and put the pot outside. He started
coffee, hunted around until he found the chocolate chips
and the walnuts, and made a batch of Toll House cookies,
which pretty much defined the limits of his expertise in the
kitchen.

When they came out of the oven, Kate shoved back her
chair and stretched her arms over her head, bending to
touch her toes. He gestured with a plate full of cookies.
She moved to the broad, padded bench that ran around
one side of the room beneath the shelves. He brought the
cookies and a mug of coffee, properly doctored. She bit
into a cookie and had to control a grunt of approval. The
coffee scalded her tongue on first sip, and she blew on it
to cool it down.

"So what do you think?"

"You never put in enough chips. Chocolate's one of the
four major food groups, you know."

The corners of his mouth twitched, and Kate realized it
was the first time she'd seen them. She decided she liked
him without a beard and was glad it hadn't been covering
up a receding chin or pouty lips or buck teeth.

"What are the other three?" he asked.

"What other three?"

He grinned to himself. "The other three major food
groups."

"Oh." She pulled herself together and dragged her attention back to her cookie. "According to Bobby, fat, salt and
sugar. All well represented here, I'm happy to report." He
laughed, and she licked chocolate from her fingers. "No
sign of the murder weapon, I suppose?"

He shook his head. "I had half a dozen people go over

the ground from sunup yesterday morning until sundown yesterday night. Nothing."

"Someone could have been taking a shot at McAniff and missed."

"And someone could have wanted to kill Lisa Getty and stumbled onto what they in their relative innocence thought was the perfect crime."

Her look was cool but she didn't deny it. She thought of something else. "Could McAniff have had two rifles?"

"No."

"You're sure?"

"I'm not sure of a goddam thing in this case, but we do have an eyewitness. Becky Jorgensen says not."

"She saw him where, inside the cabin, from another room, for how long, maybe five seconds max? Watching while he killed her husband? And then she ran and never looked back." Kate picked up another cookie and held it. "Maybe he had another rifle outside."

"Clerk at Niniltna General Store says he bought one, and only one, the day before."

"And the bullets from all the other victims match that rifle?"

"Yes."

"But not the bullet that killed Lisa."

"No."

"You're sure?"

"Ballistics ran the same check three times. Gamble ran it through CLIS twice. We're sure."

Jack got up to refill their mugs. She watched him in frowning silence.

"Well?"

She jerked her chin at the files. "Has Chopper Jim seen those?"

"He wrote half of them. It's his territory. He was in charge of the investigation."

"So he knows all this."

"Yes."

"If he's the trooper in charge, why can't he—"

"He was sleeping with her."

The generous curves of Kate's mouth compressed together into a thin line. She held back her first comment, which was profane and futile, her second, which was physically impossible, and went with her third. "If that's all it takes to be suspected of murdering Lisa Getty, we can include half the Park."

"So I hear."

"Who else was in the area that morning?"

"That we know of? Like it says in the files." Jack ticked them off one by one. "Lottie Getty. Becky Jorgensen. Lyle and Lucy Longstaff, before they died. Lisa herself. George Perry was also there but he was about five thousand feet straight up, so I don't know that he counts."

"That's it?"

"That's it."

She took another cookie. "What do you want me to do?"

He shrugged. "Do what you do best. Go in, poke around, a nudge here, a shove there. Pretty soon something will break loose."

Kate felt her temper rise. "Couldn't stay away from me, huh?"

"Not for much longer, no," Jack said.

"Missed me that much, did you?"

"More."

"You prick." She rose hastily, banging her shoulder on the shelf overhead and dislodging a dozen cassette tapes. She turned just in time to keep the deck from crashing to the floor.

Jack said the only thing a wise man could. "I'm sorry." He stood and touched her shoulder. She shrugged away and bent down to pick up the tapes, taking an inordinate amount of time sorting them into their correct order and lining them up in a neat, alphabetical row by title. He read the titles over her shoulder and shook his head admiringly. "You sure are narrow in your taste in music, Kate."

She stooped to pick up a cassette she'd missed before, and slid *Beethoven's Greatest Hits* between k.d. lang and Jake and Elwood Blues.

"You must go through the batteries," he tried again.

Still no reply.

He sighed. "I don't have to tell you the first twenty-four hours following the crime are the most important."

"No," she said, and he winced away from the deepening roughness of her ruined voice. "You don't have to tell me."

"I don't have to tell you it's been ten days on this one."

"No."

"The longer we wait to move, the greater the chance we'll never find the killer."

"Yes."

"As it is, we're probably just going through the motions. The killer's had too much time to clean up after him- or herself. All they have to do is sit tight and wait us out."

"Yes."

"But we do have to go through the motions, regardless."

"Yes."

He paused, watching her unresponsive back, her quick, deft hands, not quite so quick and deft as usual, as she rearranged her cassettes. "You'll do it, then?"

"Don't I always?"

He winced again. If she'd seen it she would have been glad. She sorted her tapes with a steadier hand, her thoughts a week away and twenty-five miles down the old railroad bed, in a stand of trees on the edge of a forty-eight-hundred-foot dirt airstrip. She had known all of those victims, some of them all her life.

Feeling restless and more than a little guilty, Jack wandered around the room. Coming to a stop in front of her desk, he looked down at the pad of paper covered with Kate's writing. Notes highlighting the important points of the case, he supposed. He wondered what she had made of it. Glancing over to see her back still turned to him,

he stretched out an exploratory finger to pull the tablet around so he could read it.

"Stewed tomatoes," he read. "Evaporated milk, green beans, white flour, whole wheat flour, oatmeal, raisins, dried apricots." It was a grocery list, a long one, with quantities listed in case lot amounts meant to last a year. Practical, he decided, was the best word to describe Kate Shugak. "Four hundred a day," he said out loud.

With an effort, Kate returned to the here and now. "Plus expenses."

He frowned a little. Her voice sounded odd. "You okay?"

"Plus expenses," she repeated.

"You got it."

There was a brief pause. "One time, you can't come to see me just to come see me?"

He shrugged. "Well. As long as you're here."

"I should make you sleep on the couch tonight."

"Yeah, you probably should. Are you going to?"

She swore at him. He laughed.

four

WHEN Kate killed the snow machine's engine, the resulting silence was broken once by the distant buzz of another snow-machine engine, a second time by the faraway yip of a dog. Mutt disdained a reply and jumped down from the back of the Jag. She looked up at Kate inquiringly, obviously ready, willing and able to get on with the job. "You look entirely too smug," Kate told her.

One of Mutt's eyebrows quirked up as if to say, *You* should talk.

"Go to hell," Kate told her.

A low, amused woof was her reply.

They had stopped in front of a large log cabin with a U.S. flag flying from a pole mounted on one corner of the roof and a satellite dish hanging from another. Kate dismounted and went inside.

The man behind the counter looked up. "Hey, Kate."

"Hey, Ralph. You filling in?"

He nodded. "Until they hire somebody permanent. Come rain, come shine, come sleet, come massacre, the mail must go through." Their eyes met. "Sorry. You here for yours?"

"All but the bills."

He grinned. "I'll see what I can do. Take me a minute, the mail plane just came."

"No hurry."

49

He rummaged through the mass of envelopes large and small, thick and thin, and she wandered down to the end of the counter and looked behind it. He raised his head. "Right here?" she said.

His hands stilled. "Yeah. Right here."

She shook her head. "Hell of a thing."

"Guy was some kind of a nut." His lips tightened. "I knew Pat Jorgensen twenty years. He was good people. He didn't deserve to die like that." Ralph paused. "You could have saved some of the taxpayer's money, out there on the road."

"So I hear."

"Shame you didn't."

"That's what people keep telling me." Her voice was a soft, torn sound.

Ralph Peabody, burly with a square red face and no hair, looked stolid but wasn't insensitive. He forbore to say more and resumed sorting through the envelopes.

"Mind if I go through?" Kate asked, nodding toward the curtained doorway that separated the tiny post office from the main body of the house.

He gave her a curious look but shrugged. "Go ahead. Becky's still in the hospital."

"Bill around?"

"Him and Betty are in Anchorage with her."

She pushed aside the curtain, a thin, flowered cotton hanging from a slender metal rod that upon closer inspection proved to be copper tubing nailed to the door's molding with carpet tacks, and walked through. She turned, still holding the curtain back. The doorway framed Ralph's bent head, the counter and the door of the post office perfectly. The miracle was that McAniff had not seen and shot Becky as she stood there, a horrified witness to her husband's murder.

Kate looked closer. There was a large stain on the floor beneath Ralph's feet. She shut her eyes briefly. She, too, had known Pat Jorgensen, for longer than Ralph, and yes,

he had been good people, and no, he had not deserved to die like that.

She let the curtain fall and turned. She was standing in the living room of the log house, a spacious room with an enormous console television dominating one corner, two worn but comfortable-looking easy chairs parked in front of it. Across from the stone fireplace sat a flowered couch long and wide enough for Pat to sleep on with room to spare. There was a multicolored afghan in clashing neon colors folded neatly over its back. Becky crocheted, Kate remembered. There wasn't a friend of hers who hadn't been presented with an afghan in colors bright enough to guarantee a headache if you looked at it long enough.

A picture window was cut into the wall facing the airstrip, with Angqaq Peak and attendant, acolyte Quilaks rising in the background. Between the strip and the mountains were the trees, clustered together like gossips fearing to move out of earshot. Above the trees she could see wisps of smoke from the chimneys of homes and businesses in Niniltna, and a large column of steam from the town's electric plant. It must have looked like shelter and sanctuary to a panicked sixty-four-year-old woman who had just seen her husband gunned down in cold blood.

Kate stepped to the main door of the house, which opened off the living room, walked through the entryway and opened the outside door. Standing at the top of the steps, she paused, looking down the length of the runway. Mutt trotted around the corner of the house and stood, looking up, tail curled in a question mark.

Across the runway from the house stood a cleared and filled section of land that supported a square, two-story building. A faded sign beneath the eaves read, "Chugach Air Taxi Service, Inc." To the building's right were tiedowns occupied by a dozen small planes, most of them still on skis. Kate came down the steps and crossed the strip to the hangar. The large sliding doors were closed. She went into the office by the side door and through it to

the hangar. A man in gray-striped coveralls was bent over the open cowling of a six-seater Cessna 206. The Cessna could have used a paint job, the man a bath.

Something metal went crunch. "Shit!" he yelled. He wound up and threw the screwdriver as hard as he could in what turned out to be Kate's direction. She ducked and it whizzed over her head. Behind her Mutt jumped and caught the screwdriver's plastic handle neatly in her teeth.

"Nice to see you, too, George," Kate said, standing straight. "What's the matter with the Loose Goose this time?"

"Damn magneto's gone again," he said glumly, "and my frigging mechanic picked now to go work repairing equipment on a fish processor in Dutch Harbor." George Perry was tall and thin with shaggy brown hair and wire-rimmed glasses, both liberally splattered with grease. He looked more like a CPA than a bush pilot, but he cursed pretty good. He was cursing when Mutt trotted over and lay the screwdriver carefully at his feet. "Thanks, Mutt," he said, stooping to pick it up with one hand and pull on Mutt's ears with the other. She stood where she was, an expression of blissful idiocy on her face. "What brings you to town, Kate?"

"Came to pick up my mail. Ralph told me you'd just brought it in. I thought I'd stop over, say hi."

He cocked his head at her. "You looking for work? I've got two groups up on the Bump already and a third coming in tomorrow. I could use another guide."

"That's right, it is that time of year."

"No shit sherlock." He gave the Cessna a damning glare. "That's why I need this old bucket of bolts up and running. So? What say? Can I put you on the payroll?"

She shook her head. "Nah. I'm almost three hundred bucks to the good this year. I can wait for the kings to hit fresh water."

He sighed. "Everybody's flush this spring. Whatever happened to the good old days, when you could count on half the Park rats drinking up their summer savings and being broke by February 1st?"

"I don't know, I guess they really are the good old days."

He eyed her with a gloomy expression. "It's your fault. You busted that bootlegger last winter and now everybody has to go to the Roadhouse. And Bernie won't let anyone mush home drunk."

"Guilty as charged," she said with a faint smile. She paused. "I hear you tried to land in the middle of the fireworks last week." He looked blank and she gestured vaguely behind her. "When McAniff went ape and shot all those people."

His face darkened. "Yes."

"Can you tell me about it?" He looked at her, surprised and a little disgusted, and she shook her head at once. "No, it's not that." She hesitated. Jack had advised discretion, but the word was going to get around sooner or later. For all she knew, the police were holding a press conference in Anchorage as she spoke. "Lisa Getty was shot by a different rifle than the rest of the victims."

It took George a moment. "A different rifle?" he asked. "You mean McAniff *didn't* shoot her?"

"No."

He looked a little at a loss. "Well then, who did?"

She shrugged. "They don't know. I'm looking into it. That's why I need to know what you saw that day."

"Jesus, Mary and Joseph," he said slowly. "You mean we got another killer still on the loose?" She nodded. "Christ." He tossed the screwdriver into the toolbox. "You want some coffee?"

"Sure."

He led the way into his office, and she sat down on the old couch, patched so many times it was hard to tell where the Naugahyde left off and the duct tape began. He handed

her a cup and sat behind his desk. "If you're working with the cops, you've probably seen my statement. I don't know what I can add to it."

Kate settled back and sipped at her coffee. It tasted like three-in-one-oil. "I've always liked 'I-was-there' stories. Just tell me what happened."

He was right; he couldn't add much more than what he'd said in his statement. The Cessna, so full of mail he'd had to take out the two back rows of seats, had been maybe a hundred yards off the south end of the airstrip when a bullet smashed into the windshield. Another hit the fuselage, by which time he'd figured out what was happening. "I thought for a minute I was back on a short final at Khe Sanh," he said, shuddering. "I pushed in the throttle and pulled the stick as far back into my lower intestine as it would go and I was outa there."

"I don't blame you," she observed. "In your statement, you say you circled for a while."

"Yeah, I got up out of range and put her into a slow turn. I saw two bodies laying out on the edge of the strip. I think I caught a glimpse of Lisa's body through the trees. You know she always wears—wore those flashy fluorescent bibs and parkas from North Face that practically glow in the dark." He took a deep breath. "And I saw a guy take off through the woods on a Polaris. All the time I'm on the radio, trying to raise the troopers. I got Chopper Jim, and he told me to go to Tok. I was happy to oblige."

"When'd you get back?"

"That evening." He shook his head. "Place was a zoo. There was about a hundred cops crawling around with all that sumbitchin' yellow tape they like to string every-where, couldn't taxi in a straight line without fouling in it to save your life. Body bags all over everywhere. Place looked like Tan Son Nhut in '68." He tried to shrug, but it turned into a shiver. "That guy McAniff was out of his fucking mind."

"Guess so," she said in a neutral voice, trying not to think of the killer lying in the slush and snow at her feet, crying because his mouth was bleeding.

George set his mug down and reached for a rag, wiping ineffectually at the grease on his hands. "It was creepy as hell, there at first. People standing around, too shocked to be angry. Cops all business, taking statements, putting everything they found in Ziploc bags. I saw one trooper bagging some snow." He paused, his eyes remote. "Everybody else was just standing around, watching. Steve Syms's girlfriend from Ahtna, what's her name—"

"Cindy. Beerbohm."

"Yeah, apparently Steve was due to fly out to see her that night. She flew in instead and had hysterics from one end of the strip to the other. Can't blame her, but it didn't help things much. Your grandma finally took her home and put her to bed."

"Yes," Kate said. "Emaa does what needs to be done."

"She is a good old gal," George agreed.

I wouldn't go that far, Kate thought.

"Everybody came from every homestead between here and Ahtna, and half Ahtna did, too. All standing around in a big circle like a herd of cows looking at something strange come into their pasture. Weird looking, you know?"

Kate nodded. It sounded depressingly like any crime scene she'd ever been at.

"They were here for days, the whole bunch of them, and then they all left, in something like ten minutes, in a couple of Twin Otters." He shook his head. "It was quiet out there for maybe a day, and then by God if they didn't all come back."

"Who all?"

"Everybody all. Cops to go over the ground again, who knows why. Everybody else came to watch the cops. I'm not sure Lottie ever did leave."

Kate stirred. "Maybe she had more cause to stay than most."

"Yeah, I know she and Lisa were pretty close. It was creepy though. She didn't move, she didn't talk. She just stood there, watching. When it got dark and the cops borrowed a generator and started stringing lights, some of the folks tried to get her to go home. I don't think she even heard them. She just stood there, like this huge statue. She looked like . . . I don't know, Lot's wife, maybe?" He gave an involuntary shudder and looked over at Kate with a sheepish expression. "Sorry. Between Cindy screaming and yelling on one side and Lottie acting like the specter at the feast on the other . . . it was, well, creepy," he repeated.

"I'll bet."

"Hell with that. You and I are alive, right?"

"Right."

"In spite of the fact that now we got us another crazy person on the loose with a gun." Kate got the impression he still didn't quite believe it, an impression confirmed by his next words. "You sure I can't talk you into a job? I got a bunch of Koreans up at the base camp. Their second time," he added. "They didn't make the summit last year."

She snorted and shook her head. "No, thanks. I never do second-timers."

He sighed. "Can't say's I blame you. They're always so friggin' determined they're gonna make it *this* time, they don't care if it's blowing a blizzard up top and you can't see a foot in front of your face." He thought. "Maybe I can get Lottie to take 'em up."

Kate hesitated in the doorway. "You think that's a good idea?"

"She's gotta eat, like the rest of us, and she's one of the best there is up on the Bump." He shrugged. "Probably be better for her to be working than sitting around the house moping."

"She might not be in the right mood to entertain," Kate suggested. "Especially now."

"She never is. But she will get my climbers up and back in one piece."

"True. I'm going up to see her when I leave here," Kate said. "Want me to tell her to check in?"

"Do that." He eyed her sharply. "She know yet?" Kate shook her head. "And you get to tell her. That's not a job I'd wish on my worst enemy. Well, tell her I'll be gone this afternoon but I'll be back here tomorrow morning, and to look me up if she wants the job."

Kate walked down the airstrip and a little way into the stand of trees, and halted. She stood very still, looking around. There were birch and diamond willow and alder and cottonwood and scrub spruce. The branches of the deciduous trees were as yet leafless, but their bark was beginning to darken over the subcutaneous flow of running sap. The evergreens were thickly needled and a deep, dark green, except at the tip of each branch, where spring was beginning to emerge in a new growth of lighter green. It looked the very picture of serene renewal, not at all a scene for massacre, or for cold-blooded, opportunistic murder.

She looked up and could barely see the sky through the branches tangled overhead. It was silly, she knew, but Kate suddenly felt as if she were intruding where she was not wanted. There was an almost conscious feeling of resistance, a feeling of . . . what? Possessiveness? A hoarding of secrets hardly won?

She shook herself. At this rate, her imagination would be putting in for overtime. Hearing a plane in the distance, she collected her mail and headed up the river at a decorous pace. She was not looking forward to her next interview.

Next to Lottie, Kate felt dainty. Next to Lottie Getty, Sasquatch would have felt dainty. Lottie was big, six feet

tall in her stocking feet, and weighed in at a hundred and ninety pounds, most of it muscle from years of hauling nets and packing game out through the bush. Her features were an odd contrast to the rest of her; she had large, widely spaced eyes of an innocent blue, fair skin showing not half her forty years, and a way of walking and talking slow that led the uninitiated into thinking she thought slow as well.

"Hi, Lottie." At first Kate thought Lottie wasn't going to let her in. After a long, tense pause, Lottie stepped back and motioned her inside. Another wave of the hand directed her toward a worn easy chair sitting to one side of an old iron wood stove that Lottie's father must have brought with him when he came to the Park in '52. Kate sat down, got back up again and removed a box of rifle shells, a Prince William Sound tide-book, a half-eaten, molding Hostess fruit pie, a photograph album, a tattered Harlequin romance and a gray cat, and sat back down.

Lottie sat opposite her, large, silent, impassive. Kate let her eyes wander around the interior of the cabin. It was larger than her own. The loft was enclosed, with a proper staircase leading up to it, doors led off a hallway in the back of the house, and the kitchen was separated from the living room by a counter lined with stools. Every available horizontal surface was covered with the detritus of bush life; Kate saw a dismantled beaver trap on the kitchen counter, with fur still stuck to the jaws. A dozen or more rifles, from a petite and, if the shine of its stock were any indication, brand new twenty-two to a silver-mounted over-and-under 12-gauge-30.06 combination were stacked in racks nailed to every available vertical surface. Knives in leather scabbards dangled next to the rifles, salmon filleting knives with white plastic grips, skinning knives with handles of some kind of antler, what looked like a Bowie knife with a handle intricately carved from fossil ivory. A mounted moose head hung over the

wood stove, and caribou, goat and sheep heads festooned the other walls, most with coats, mittens and more knives hung from their racks. Any wall that dared show a bare face to the world had been promptly veiled with a dusty hide; black bear, brown bear, wolf, wolverine, coyote, an unexpected rattlesnake.

A wooden rocking chair with a splintered seat sat next to a couch, patched like George's where the springs had come through, this one with black electrician's tape. From what she could see of the kitchen, Kate didn't think the table had been cleared or the dishes washed in months. Every corner of the room was filled; with spiderwebs on the ceiling and dust balls on the floor.

The house looked like Fairbanks after the flood and before the cleanup. A movement caught the corner of her eye; the gray cat was sitting at her feet with her tail curled around her paws, watching Kate with large, unblinking green eyes. "I'm not moving," Kate told her, although she did sympathize. The chair she was sitting in was, so far as she could see, the only place in the house where one could sit down in relative comfort.

The cat yawned and began to wash. She could wait.

"I heard you caught him," a voice like a dull knife said. It took Kate a moment to realize it was Lottie's voice.

She looked up and met the wide blue stare. "Yes," she said. "I did."

"You should have killed him when you had the chance."

"So I've been told," Kate said steadily.

"But you didn't."

"No."

"But you got him."

"Yes."

There was a long pause. "At least you got him," Lottie said, still in that dull voice.

"Lottie," Kate said, and stopped. How to say it? she thought, and tried again. "I wanted to stop by and see how you were."

"Why?"

Kate floundered. "We grew up together. Lisa and I went through school together. I just thought—"

"We've never been that close," Lottie pointed out.

"Not since school, no." Kate bit her lip. "I'm sorry about Lisa, though. You lived together all your lives. It must hurt like hell."

Lottie's face remained blank, a caricature china doll. For lack of something better to do, Kate leaned forward to pick up the photograph album she had removed from the chair. The gray cat had curled up on it, and her green eyes promised retribution for this second disruption of her morning nap. "May I?" Lottie said nothing, and Kate opened the album and began to leaf through it. "God, some of these are old. Look at these . . . what did they call them? Tintypes?"

"Sepia prints," Lottie said. She rose and drifted over to stand behind Kate's shoulder.

"Who's this hunk? Wow. He looks like Charles Lindbergh."

"My grandfather." Lottie paused, and then said almost reluctantly, "My mother's father."

"Nice smile. You look kind of like him."

"He was a prick," Lottie said flatly. "He was a drunk. My mother told me she eloped with my father because my father was the first person who ever said he loved her."

Kate's hands stilled for a moment before turning the page. "Who's this with the hat? Thing must've weighed ten pounds with all those ruffles and bows."

"My great-grandmother."

Kate peeled away the transparency and looked at the back of the picture. She whistled. "This picture was taken in 1900." She squinted again at it. "You look kind of like her, too." She turned the page and laughed. "There must be six yards of fabric in that old nightgown, or whatever it is, and look at all those tiny buttons on his boots. That kid looks so clean he could squeak. Bet he stayed that way for

about five minutes." Kate could feel Lottie leaning over her shoulder, and she paged forward. "These clothes look World War Two-ish; these must be your parents. Weird colors."

"Tinted."

"Right." Kate flipped through more pages, and slowed down. "Lisa?"

"Yes."

Kate frowned a little. "Where is she? I don't recognize the place."

A pause. "The first five summers of our lives we spent out at the cannery on Mummy Island."

Kate looked again and couldn't help smiling. "Lisa sure didn't like clothes much, did she?"

"No." A pause. "The cannery superintendent was always calling Mom to tell him Lisa had her clothes off again and was running around the dock naked."

Kate kept her eyes fixed on the page. "And where are you?"

"Over there. In back and to the left."

"With your clothes on."

Somehow the joke fell flat. "Yes."

Kate's finger ran down to the bottom of the page. "Your mother and father. That's you on your father's lap?"

"Yes. One of the few times he could bear to touch his fat, dumb kid."

Kate turned the page and said with relief, "School pictures! Were we ever really that young?"

The pictures of the two sisters, arranged chronologically and side by side, showed a maturing process far kinder to the younger sister than to the elder. Lisa ripened. Lottie weathered. Lisa grew from a plump baby cuteness to a girlish prettiness to real beauty. Lottie just grew, taller and wider. Lisa was slender, and there was a lissome quality to her form, in the way her golden scarf of hair lay on her shoulders, in the bend of her long, slender neck, in the graceful disposal of her arms, that made her look as

if she were moving even as she posed for a still picture. Lottie in her pictures seemed rooted, immobile, static, her body massive and graceless. Lisa's eyes sparkled, her cheeks dimpled, her smile was wide and filled with a secret glee that made one wonder what was so amusing. Kate remembered the effect to be even more irritating in person.

She looked until the end of the album, but she never found a single picture of Lottie smiling. As near as Kate could tell, Lottie had been born with a scowl. Or no, not a scowl, that was too strong. Maybe she just never learned to smile, which wasn't quite the same thing. Through the years, her face only became squarer and more stolid. There was no secret fun in Lottie's face, no mischief, in fact little animation of any kind. What struck Kate most was the quality of speechless endurance in that static expression.

She looked up and saw it repeated in the face across from her, and closed the album with a snap. "Thanks for letting me look at this," she said out loud. "I like looking at old pictures, don't you?"

"No."

You must have had the album out for some reason, Kate thought, but refrained from saying so. Although, looking around, she wasn't sure anything in this house was ever really put away. "Was Lisa seeing anybody when she . . . Was there someone special lately?"

Lottie's lips twisted in a humorless travesty of a smile. "When wasn't there?"

"Anyone in particular?"

"What's it to you?"

"Just wondering, Lottie," Kate said in a level voice. In a way she was relieved at Lottie's hostility; anything was better than that inanimate, somehow faceless shell. "I knew she was seeing Chopper Jim," she lied.

"Who wasn't seeing him, at one time or another?"

"Well, there's me," Kate said, smiling.

The shell seemed to crack a little. "That's right. I remember, you never did much like standing in line."

"And then there's you, so that makes two of us." Kate tried without success to see through the crack in the shell to what was beneath.

"Lisa's thing with Jim ended in February." Lottie's voice was without expression.

"Anyone since then?"

"It's nobody's business if there was or there wasn't," Lottie said, her fists clenching. "None of it matters now. Lisa's dead. Why don't you just butt out?"

Lottie was entitled to her grief, and suddenly Kate felt disgusted with her intrusion into that grief. "I'm sorry, Lottie," she said, rising to her feet. From the corner of one eye she caught a glimpse of a gray streak and turned to see the cat curling into a neat ball in the warm place Kate's bottom had left. Kate smiled and turned to share it with Lottie. There was no response from that bleak face. "I'm sorry," Kate repeated, her smile fading. "Oh yeah, I saw George Perry on my way out here. He told me to tell you he needs a guide for a party of Koreans climbing Angqaq."

"North or south peak?"

"He didn't say. They're two-timers, though. George said to stop by the hangar tomorrow morning if you're interested." Kate gestured at the foil-wrapped package she'd carried in with her. "I brought you some bread. Just baked a batch last week."

Without expression Lottie jerked her thumb at the kitchen table, and obediently Kate walked over to it.

The table wasn't just crowded with the detritus of life; it was stacked with casserole dishes, none of them touched. Some were just beginning to go green on top.

"Why do people always bring food?" Lottie said from behind her.

Kate shrugged. "I don't know. Because they want to

do something, and it's something to do." She hesitated, almost spoke, and thought, The hell with it. It can wait. She turned and went to the door.

"Kate," Lottie said.

Kate paused and looked over her shoulder.

"Why?" Lottie said. "Why did he do it?" She took a step forward and repeated in that earnest, little-girl voice, "Can you tell me why?"

With her hand on the knob, Kate debated with the grain of the wood in the door for a reply. "I don't know, Lottie. Who knows what's going on in the head of someone like that? He's just another crazy. They happen along sometimes." She looked up and sucked in her breath.

Lottie's pale features seemed blunted somehow, bludgeoned by circumstance into numb acceptance. "Why?" she repeated, looking directly at Kate for the first time. "Why did he do it?"

Kate, abashed in the presence of so much grief and pain and rage, shook her head without replying. She had no answers for Lottie.

Outside, Mutt nudged her head against Kate's hand, but Kate stood where she was, listening. There was no sound from inside the house, nothing to indicate that Lottie had descended from her mountain of grief. Kate turned to her left and went around to the back, moving quietly along the slippery paths.

The backyard of the Getty homestead looked pretty much like her own, although much less neat. A tumble of empty, rusting fifty-five-gallon drums and five-gallon Blazo tins stood heaped beneath a concealing, albeit rapidly melting, layer of snow. There was an open garage filled with hand tools, a small tractor, a snow machine with a trailer attached, and an old ceramic toilet bowl, minus the tank. There were two small windows over the workbench, both of them so festooned with cobwebs and

years of grime that the light they shed on the inside was negligible.

In front of the barn, hands in her pockets, Kate stared around, her gaze unfocused, letting the feel of the place sink in. It was like a hundred other homesteads all over the Alaskan bush. There was a food cache, a fuel cache, a woodpile, a generator shack and a barn, none of which contained anything out of the ordinary. There was even a satellite dish on the roof of the main house, and Kate wondered idly how much it cost in fuel to run the generator through the winter. She'd given some thought to installing a dish herself, if only for MTV and VH-1 and the Nashville Network.

A honking wedge of Canadian geese flew into view. They were early, but there were a few newly opened leads in the marsh next to Niniltna. It definitely was spring.

Her eyes followed the flock and caught in a thinning of the treetops behind the barn. She walked around and found a greenhouse, close to and not much smaller than the barn, built of two-by-fours and plastic siding. A profusion of greenery showed through the translucent walls. From the outside, the tall plants filling up the interior in leafy profusion looked like tomato plants.

From the inside, they did not.

"Son of a bitch," Kate said, more in sorrow than in anger.

She returned to the barn and pulled and shoved her way into the clutter, making no attempt to keep her activities quiet. She moved a crate of eggs to one side, lifted a sack of potatoes into a corner and boosted a barrel of flour which the mice had found before her onto the crate. She found what she was looking for stacked high in the far right corner, beneath a lashed-down tarp.

She came out of the barn beating the dust out of her clothes and looked up to find Lottie watching her, mute. Kate didn't apologize. She jerked her head toward the greenhouse. "Did you know? Were you partners?" Lottie

said nothing, and Kate forgot about shielding Lottie from the news. "Lottie, McAniff didn't shoot Lisa." The other woman's head snapped up, and Kate nodded grimly. "That's right. The police ran a test on the bullets they found. They know that the one that killed Lisa came from a different gun."

Lottie didn't move, didn't speak; her expression didn't change. It infuriated Kate. "Lottie! If you two were wholesaling dope out of your backyard, any fights you had with one-time or potential customers give us one hell of a list of suspects! Who were you selling to?"

When Lottie still didn't answer, Kate, exasperated, went to her and shook her. It was like trying to shake Angqaq Peak. "Talk to me!"

Lottie's face seemed to crumple, her voice to shrink. Kate had to strain to hear her. "What?" she said. "What did you say?"

Again the stumbling, shrunken voice. "Are you going to tell?"

"Oh hell," Kate said, disgusted, and left.

five

SHE could hear the noise from Bobby's house all the way down to where Squaw Creek joined the Kanuyaq River. Its main component seemed to be stentorian male voices doing a lot of whooping and yelling of song lyrics that were faint but audible, even above the noise of the Jag's engine, and which grew steadily louder as she approached the house. Just to be on the safe side, Kate parked the Jag down by the creek and walked the remaining distance to the ramp that led up to the front door.

It was a large cedar A-frame, its roof festooned with a writhing cluster of wiring that led to a 112-foot metal tower rising starkly up out of the backyard like the skeleton of a spaceship. Mounted on the tower were two white drumlike apparatuses facing west and south. A satellite TV dish, pointing low on the Alaskan horizon to pick up equatorial-orbit satellite transmissions, hung precariously from a crossbar above and behind the microwave shots. Antennae of one kind or another took up what little space there was left, and the whole thing looked top-heavy and Leaning Tower of Pisa-ish.

The closer Kate came the louder the noise got, and the less melodic the singing. Country Joe McDonald and the Fish were leading the chorus in a verse urging mothers to be the first one on their block to have their boy come home

in a box. Normally Kate would have opened the door without knocking and gone in. Today something told her this might be unwise.

The music stopped abruptly, and from inside the house somebody yelled, "Hey, Bobby, I think it's time to call it down." There was a deafening avalanche of approving raspberries, oinks and rebel yells.

"Okay, okay, you guys," Kate heard Bobby say in his customary roar. Mutt, standing next to her, recognized his voice and her ears went up and she looked at Kate with a quizzical expression. Kate sat down on the porch railing and prepared to listen to Bobby call whatever it was down. Mutt, knowing what was waiting for her in Bobby's wood box next to the fireplace inside, sat down herself with a disgruntled thump. There was a kind of rustling from inside the house, as if many were arranging themselves to listen, and then Bobby's big bass voice, fifty decibels lower than it generally was and unnaturally solemn, began to speak.

"January 30, 1968," he intoned. "Tet, the Asian Lunar New Year, begins. The VC break into dry cleaners and steal ARVN uniforms to wear during the attack. They bring out hidden weapons and test-fire them during the holiday fireworks." He paused. "That night, it begins. The VC attack a hundred major cities and towns in the Central Highlands and Lowlands of South Vietnam."

Someone screamed. There was no other word for it, and it was instantly answered by other screams rising together in a single, united, animal howl. Mutt was instantly on her feet, ears back, yellow eyes wide and alarmed. With a hand she noticed was shaking a little, Kate smoothed the hair down on the back of her neck and patted Mutt's head.

Bobby's voice resumed. "January 31, Day 2. The VC attack in Saigon, Hue and the Mekong Delta. They attack and hold the American embassy in Saigon for six hours against Marine counterattack. In two weeks, the VC fights its way into every town and village in South Vietnam." Bobby paused. "Westmoreland calls for 206,000 more

troops and another 15 tactical fighter squadrons."

There was another chorus, one of whistles and jeers and boos. "But hey, hey, LBJ, how many kids did you kill today goes on television and says there is light at the end of the tunnel!" somebody yelled.

Bobby raised his voice over the resulting uproar. "March 16. My Lai." Silence. "That same day, Bobby Kennedy announces he's going to run for president."

Someone made a rude comment concerning Marilyn Monroe, and the animals were back in force.

"March 22. LBJ relieves Westmoreland."

The rafters of Bobby's house resounded with cheers.

"And on March 31, hey, hey, LBJ, how many kids did you kill today withdraws from the 1968 presidential race!"

This time the cheering thundered through the cedar logs and up through the deck of the porch, joyless and unrestrained, a wall of raging sound. Mutt couldn't stand it and began to bark, and Kate locked a restraining hand in the fur of her ruff.

"We were there!" Bobby roared. "We were at Hue!"

"The City of Perfect Peace!"

"Sometimes you have to destroy a city to save it!"

"We were at the embassy in Saigon!"

"Send in the spooks to lead the counterattack!"

"Yeah! The fucking CIA oughta be good for something!"

"Spear carrier!"

"Cannon fodder!"

"Ass wipe!"

"*Yeah!*"

"We were at Da Nang!"

"Khe Sanh!"

"The ghost of Dien Bien Phu!"

"Nha Trang!"

"Tan Son Nhut!" Unsurprised, Kate heard a voice she recognized as George Perry's. "The battle for the body bags!"

"Yeah!"

"Gentlemen," Bobby roared, "here's to promotion through attrition!"

"Hear, hear!"

"Here's to the fucking Five O'Clock Follies!"

"Body count! We want a body count!"

"Briefing by Colonel Blimp!"

"Here's to the fucking light at the fucking end of the fucking tunnel!"

"Fucking A!"

"Here's to 206,000 more troops and another 15 tactical fighter squadrons!"

"And to another 30 MIAs!"

"Here's to fragging the fuckers up front!"

There was an unexpected pause, into which came a voice that sounded aggrieved and a little bewildered. "But we *won*," he insisted. "We *won* Tet."

Someone must have hit the Play button on the stereo. The tape slipped a little, and then picked up in the middle of the song, singing whoopee we're all going to die. Someone began stamping his feet, they all joined in, and again the floor of the porch began to shake.

"Didn't we?" the voice said sadly, a plaintive question that reached Kate clearly through the door. "Didn't we win?"

The door jerked open. A sepulchral voice announced, "This is the end." Kate took an involuntary step backward.

The doorman had smeared black makeup beneath his eyes and wore combat fatigues fraying at knees and elbows. In one hand he held a half-empty bottle of mescal, still with worm; with the other he raised a joint to his lips and sucked in. Kate didn't know him. She backed up another step and gave an ingratiating and, she hoped, nonthreatening smile. "I'm looking for Bobby."

He looked at her without expression. Behind him the singing continued unabated.

"Who is it, Max?" A voice came from behind him. The owner of the voice wheeled into Kate's view.

"Well, hey, gorgeous!" Bobby roared. With a single shove he sent his wheelchair sliding down the ramp, and with a flick of large-knuckled, clever hands turned himself sideways and slid to a hockey stop in a shower of wet, grainy snow. He looked up at her with a grin. "Come to celebrate the retaking of Hue with us?"

"Bobby, I'm sorry," she told him, "I completely forgot what time of year it was. You want me out of here?"

He waved an expansive hand. "No problem. The Fifth Annual Twentieth Anniversary Celebration of the Tet Offensive is open to anybody, especially good-looking round eyes." He leered at her on his way back up the ramp, and she jumped out of the way. Bobby Clark drove his wheelchair like an offensive weapon.

The fatigue-clad figure holding the joint at shoulder arms hung around the perimeter like a green-and-brown ghost. His eyes were deeply set and vacant, the pupils dilated out to the edge of the iris. "Excuse me," Bobby said, "you met Max Chaney yet? No? Max Chaney, Kate Shugak. He works for Dan O'Brian; he's the ranger took Miller's place."

"Oh." Kate held out a hand. "Hi, nice to meet you."

"My only friend, the end," Max Chaney replied. He took another toke, pulling the smoke deep into his lungs, and without exhaling vanished back into the house. Kate only hoped he didn't swell up and explode.

"Ah, never mind him, poor bastard's carrying a hell of a load, what with—" A rifle went off somewhere. "Goddammit, you guys," Bobby roared, a bellow that echoed around the clearing and off the treetops. "I told you to cut that shit out! Everybody's jumpy enough with that craziness week before last! Cut it out!" There was no reply; neither were there any more rifle shots.

"What brings you here, sweetcakes?" Bobby waggled rakish eyebrows. "Am I about to get lucky?"

"You wish," she retorted. Affronted at being ignored, Mutt reared up and laved Bobby's face with a damp and loving tongue.

"Goddam, woman," Bobby roared, "you brung the wolf with you! How many times I gotta tell you, no goddamn wolves in the house!" He cuffed Mutt on the head. She grinned up at him, tongue lolling out of the side of her mouth.

"Well, get outa the friggin' doorway, you're blocking traffic," he grumbled, shoving open the door. Kate was almost blown back by the blast of sound. With a single push of powerful black forearms, Bobby whizzed over to the stereo and turned it down. There were protests, which he quelled with a single roar. "Shut the hell up, you noisy bastards! We got company!"

Half a dozen men looked up from various sprawling positions about the room. They were all in their early forties and dressed alike in jeans and T-shirts, some with fatigue caps, some with olive-drab jackets. The air was layered thickly with the smells of dope and alcohol and cigarettes.

Mutt made a beeline for the wood box. She nosed and pawed her way down through the kindling and the split logs and struck gold, bringing up a bone that looked vaguely mooselike in character and still had bits of meat and gristle clinging to it. She sat down at once to gnaw.

"Mutt!" Kate said, shocked. "Where are your manners?"

Mutt, without releasing her grip on the bone, rose and trotted over to rear up with both forepaws on the arms of Bobby's chair. She didn't quite know how to go about discharging her debt of gratitude without dropping the bone, and this she was clearly unwilling to do, so she growled around it as affectionately as she was able, causing several of the men to move closer to the door.

"Goddam, woman," Bobby roared, fending her off,

"get this goddam wolf offa me!"

Kate grinned and signaled Mutt down. "Goddam, woman!" Bobby roared again. "I don't know why I let either of you in the goddam house!"

"Me, either," somebody said.

Kate knew that voice. "Bernie?"

A tall, skinny man with long, thinning hair bound back in a ponytail looked up from a Nintendo Game Boy. "Hey, Kate."

"Wait a minute," she said. "Wait just a damn minute here. I know for a fact you weren't in Vietnam."

"Nope," Bernie agreed peacefully. "I was in the mall."

Kate was mystified and looked it. "The mall?"

Bernie took pity on her. "The Washington, D.C. mall, in 1970, in company with about a million other people. I was also among the three thousand John Mitchell honored with tossing behind a chicken-wire fence for twenty-four hours, in direct contravention of our first amendment rights." He thought, his brow creasing. "Or was it fourth amendment? I was never really sure."

"A campus commando," Bobby told Kate, not without affection.

"Nope." Bernie gulped down the rest of his beer. The Game Boy beeped indignantly at him and he looked back at it. "Just somebody with a low lottery number, not enough stroke to get in the National Guard, and a distaste for tropical climates."

"Max Chaney you met," Bobby said, "and you know Jeff."

Jeff Talbot, a dark, lithe man who contrived to look dapper in blue jeans and a gray wool shirt, snapped a salute and grinned at Kate. "U.S. Marine guard, American embassy, Saigon. At your service, ma'am."

His eyes wandered over her in lingering fashion, but she knew that with Jeff it was more genetic imperative than implied insult and she ignored it. "Hi, George," she said to the pilot.

"Hey, Kate," George said, waving a beer bottle at her. "Long time no see."

"George was at Ton Son Nhut. Demetri Totemoff, Nha Trang, and Pete Kvasnikof, Pleiku."

"Hi, Kate, how's Jack?" Pete inquired.

"He's fine," Kate replied.

"I'll just bet he is, now," Pete said, but he said it to himself.

"Okay, guys," Bobby said, " 'bout time to break this party up and run you off."

There were groans and grumbles of protest.

"Hey, whaddaya want?" he demanded. "We done sung the 'Feel Like I'm Fixin' to Die Rag.' At least three of you got wives, and, Jeff, I know for a fact you can't go twenty-four hours without getting laid; your pecker'll shrivel up and die on you."

"Can't have that," Jeff said with his quick grin. He stood and drained his beer. "Thanks, Bobby," he said, reaching down a hand. "Good one, this year."

"Yeah." They did a jive handshake, complete with high and low fives, and Jeff left. The starting of his snow machine outside acted like a signal to the rest of the group, and one by one they lined up to thank Bobby and make their goodbyes.

"I'll be out to the Roadhouse to visit tomorrow," Kate told Bernie.

"Good." He gave her shoulder a poke. "See you then."

Max Chaney stuck out his hand, missing Bobby's by about a foot, stared right through Kate and drifted out the door like smoke. "Is he driving?" she asked Bobby in a low voice.

"Nah. He flew down from the Step yesterday and Pete brought him out."

"Good." When the door closed behind Max, the last to leave, Kate inquired, "How'd it go this year?"

"All right." Bobby began emptying ashtrays into the

garbage. "It's getting to be less like work and more like fun."

"About time." Kate found the broom and began sweeping.

He looked up and said soberly, "Some of those guys have some awful goddam tough ghosts to exorcise. You're too young and you weren't there. You don't know."

"I've been known to crack a book or two, and I've been listening to you for thirteen years," she pointed out.

"You don't know," he repeated.

It was true, and Kate was glad of it. "You seem relatively sane."

"I'm one of the lucky ones. I buried my ghosts with my legs," he said, without bitterness.

"What's so lucky about loosing your legs?"

"I was in the hospital for months. I had the chance to decompress. The other guys were in the jungle one day and in downtown San Francisco being called baby killers the next." He shook his head. "Grunt Rule Number 1. Never lose a war if you can help it. It upsets the folks back home."

She paused in her sweeping and looked at him. "So, when you throw a party like this, you're helping them to decompress?"

He shrugged. "We hang out, have a few beers, smoke a few joints, remember, talk, listen to music, yell, scream. Sometimes we pound on each other a little. We let off steam, take the edge off."

"Hasn't the edge dulled a little by now? It's been twenty-plus years."

"For some, yes, For some, no. For some on some days, yes. For some on some days, no."

"When I was little, I remember my father and Abel talking—"

He shook his head. "No, Kate. They were Class of '45. Different thing."

"Different how? They got shot at, their friends died."

"They came home to a parade, and a G.I. bill, and job preference, and if that wasn't enough, the Nuremburg trials showed them beyond a doubt that they'd fought the essence of evil and won."

"Bobby," she said, "something I've always wanted to ask you. Sometimes you talk like y'all was raised in the middle of the Okefenokee Swamp, and at others you seem to have just sauntered out of Harvard Yard. What gives?"

He grinned at her, a teasing grin, and she knew that was the only answer she was going to get. "Okay," she said, resigned, "then tell me what Bernie gets out of coming to the Tet Annual?"

"Are you kidding? He looks at all of us and renders up thanks to the powers that be that he ran for Canada." He paused. "And we look at him and wish we had." After a moment Bobby grinned again, a trifle lopsided this time. "And this year, with that goddam McAniff blasting away at everything that moved, we needed it. It was definitely getting a little weird out. God knows we've had about all the weird we can take." He paused. "Sometimes . . ."

"What?"

He looked at her, but his dark eyes were fixed on events long ago and far away, on a story that did not begin "once upon a time." "Sometimes, when another movie comes out, or they start up another program on television, or do another documentary on the vets, you get to feeling like you're never going to be able to clean the smell of the jungle off you." His forehead creased, and he said in a low voice, "It's a funny thing, Kate. I can still smell it. I can still taste it. You can taste death, you know. At Hue, the siege lasted a month. The bodies most of the time just stayed where they fell, and rotted there. You could smell them every time you inhaled. You could taste it in your rations, drink it from your canteen. It was the last thing you smelled at night, the first thing you smelled in the morning. It was all around you. You couldn't get away from it, and you wouldn't, until you made more of it, until

you'd killed enough people dead so that there was no one left to die."

It was the first time in their thirteen-year friendship she'd ever heard Bobby talk about the war. Kate blinked her eyes clear and said nothing.

"So," Bobby said briskly, reaching for the last over-flowing ashtray, "that's pretty much it. Once a year we get together and get a little tanked and cuss the brass and the dopes in D.C., and remember the guys who didn't make it, and cheer the fact we did." He grinned at her. "It relaxes the tension better than a good massage."

Kate cast around for an equally lighthearted response. "That new ranger, whatsisname, Chaney, didn't seem any too relaxed to me."

"Yeah, well, he was higher'n two kites, and besides, he's recovering from more'n the Nam."

"Like what? Danny boy assign him to taking the trash out of the Park?"

Bobby looked up and he wasn't smiling. "He had a thing going with Lisa Getty." Mistaking Kate's sudden stillness, Bobby said, "Yeah, I know, who didn't have a thing going with Lisa Getty. But he was new in the Park and he didn't know that, and she wasn't done with him, so he thinks it was true love, and now his heart's broken." Bobby paused. "Did I ever tell you, I got a little of that?"

Kate was momentarily diverted and even a little shocked. "Bobby. You're kidding, right?"

"Nope. Happened about ten, eleven years ago. Just after I got the roof on, she come visiting with a housewarming gift." He grinned, and it was a very wide, very male grin. "Herself. I don't think we got out of bed for a week. Swearta God, she was the all-time best piece of ass I ever had." He caught her eye and added hastily, "Except for you, of course."

"Oh, of course." Kate couldn't help herself; she laughed out loud. "Oh, Bobby. Well, I'm glad you enjoyed your-self, but I thought you had better taste."

"Yeah, well. She wasn't easy to say no to, once she'd made up her mind."

"What happened?"

"Oh, she stayed as long as it took to satisfy her curiosity about what it was like to fuck a black gimp, and then she split." He saw her look. "Come on, Kate. We both know what Lisa was like. Don't go all *nil nisi bonum* on me now."

She shook her head. "No. I just—I don't like the thought of her using you."

"Why not?" He smirked. "I used her, sure as hell, as well and as hard and for as long as I could. Didn't mean anything, but it sure felt good, and I was tired of shingling, anyway."

"Bobby, no woman is safe from you."

"You should know," he retorted.

"Mmm." She smiled at him in a way that made him forget what Lisa Getty looked like, and resumed sweeping. "So Max Chaney was seeing Lisa, was he? Since when?"

"God, I don't know. Couldn't have been for more than two-three months or she would have dropped him."

That fit with what Jack had told her about Lisa and Chopper Jim. "Where was Chaney?" she said. "The day she was killed, I mean?"

"I don't know. Up on the Step at Park HQ, I guess." He shrugged. "I didn't ask."

Kate murmured some response and worked her way into the corner behind the wood box.

Bobby regarded her back thoughtfully. "What are you doing in town, Kate?"

"Why?" she asked, without turning.

"Because it does just occur to me to wonder why you would be interested in Max's whereabouts that day." She said nothing. "Come on, Kate, what's going on? You caught the guy who killed that bunch, Lisa included, caught him fair and square your own self, yet here you are, picking my brain about Lisa and Max." He pursed his lips. "Unless, maybe—"

The broom halted, and she regarded her toes with an interest bordering on fascination. "Unless maybe what?"

She heard him shift in his chair, heard a faint squeak of rubber wheels on hardwood floor and moved her interesting toes out of the way just in time. She couldn't avoid his bright, direct gaze. "No bullshit now, Kate," he said, his drawl gone and all his verbs in their right places. "Was someone else shooting that day?"

"Yes."

"And did that someone else kill Lisa Getty?"

"Yes." Kate stepped back, swept her pile of dust and butts and potato chip and pretzel fragments into a neat pile and reached for the dustpan.

Bobby put it into her hand. "What was that crack Pete made? 'How is Jack?' Jack's in the Park?"

"He was."

"When?"

"Sunday and Monday. He flew out again this morning." She handed him the full dustpan, and he emptied it into the garbage and handed it back.

"Nice work if you can get it," Bobby observed.

"Thank you."

"You're welcome. He didn't come just to see you, though, did he?"

"No."

Bobby lost what little patience he had. "Am I going to have to drag it out of you? What'd he say?"

Kate refilled the dustpan and straightened. "He said the coroner says the bullet that killed Lisa Getty came from a different rifle than the bullets that killed the rest of the massacre victims."

"What's McAniff say?"

"He says he killed them all. Jack says McAniff was more than a little insulted at the mere suggestion that he might've missed one."

"Jesus."

She nodded. "I know. Creepy guy."

"No shit." He stretched out one large, calloused hand, and she put her own into it. He drew her over to the couch, hoisted himself into it and pulled her down next to him. Taking her hand again, he played with her fingers. "Okay, woman. Tell Bobby all about it."

She did, from Mutt's apprehension of McAniff to Jack's report on the autopsies to her own vigil at the end of the airstrip to her interview with George, and finished up with an account of her visit to Lottie's house. He listened attentively, without comment, until she told him about the greenhouse. "All dope?" he said.

She nodded. "All of it."

"How many plants'd you say?" he asked with a faraway look in his eye.

She suppressed a smile. "About seven to ten at hard labor's worth."

He sighed. "Oh well, it was just a thought."

"Besides, you're through with all that," she pointed out and waited.

In vain, because he just grinned at her. She shook her head at him.

"So that's it?" he asked, and she nodded. "Who can I tell?"

"Keep it quiet, for now. I told George the same."

"Somebody tell Lottie?"

She nodded. "Me. Today. And I'm telling you now because I want one person I trust to know where I am and what I'm doing at all times, just in case."

Bobby was pleased, and preened a little. "Why, of course. Do I get to help this time?"

"Sure." He looked delighted, and she added, "Bend your powerful brain to rounding up the usual suspects."

"Gotcha." He seemed to ripple to attention, like a cat at a mouse hole readying to pounce. "Sam Spade at your service, darling. What are we looking for?"

"The usual, Sam. Motive, means, opportunity. I'm sure Jack would appreciate some hard evidence."

"That doesn't sound very optimistic."

"We're on an old, cold trail."

"It ain't even been two weeks!" Bobby roared.

"Most crimes are solved in the first twenty-four hours," she told him. "After that the chances of finding whodunit decrease geometrically, I think by the minute. Maybe even the second."

"What do you want, to find the killer standing over the corpse with a smoking gun in his hand?"

"It could be a her."

"It surely could," Bobby said dryly. "Two-thirds of the wives and most of the girlfriends in the Park had motive. This dope business bothers me, too. You know I don't miss much, Kate."

"I know. It's why I love you."

"Down, girl." He was almost purring. "I did miss the fact that Lisa was dealing dope."

"We don't know that she was dealing."

He gave her a tolerant look. "Lottie and Lisa smoking all day, every day for a year couldn't finish off that much weed all by themselves. No, Kate, they were selling it. And if they were selling it, somebody was buying it. And you know how druggies have this tendency to wig out every now and then." His eyes lingered on the scar at her throat.

"Yes," she said flatly. "I know."

"Could have been a dissatisfied customer."

She got up and paced back and forth with long, thoughtful strides. She was between him and the fireplace and he admired the way the flames outlined her form. "What's wrong?" he said.

She paused and looked at him. "The whole thing's just so damn opportune."

He snapped his fingers. "Opportunity, the third thing we're looking for."

"Yeah." She resumed pacing. "I mean, there's McAniff, blasting away with a 30.06 at everything that moves, and somebody else just happens to be laying

for Lisa, in the same place, with another 30.06? How could they know that he'd be using a 30.06?"

"Did they know?" Bobby asked, sounding skeptical.

She halted. "You're right, they didn't have to. All they really needed was somebody else shooting, to cover the sound of their shots. By the time the difference in rifles was discovered, they'd be long gone. And were."

Bobby nodded. "A 30.06 is standard armament in the Park. If it comes to that, I've never seen you without yours, either on the rack in the back of your pickup or in a scabbard on your snow machine."

"True." Kate sat back down. "It'd be nice to have some place to start in this mess."

"Well. The means we got."

"Not in hand."

"No, but we know how it was done and with what," Bobby said, "thirty-ought-six, same as the others, only different." He stroked his chin, looking as if he wished he had a meerschaum pipe to puff on. He jerked his head. "You need to use the radio to talk to Jack?"

"Got nothing to say to him yet. Might need to, later. I hope so, anyway."

"No problem. KL7CC's—"

"I know. KL7CC's always awake."

He grinned. "Need a place to sleep?"

She grinned back. "Uh-huh."

"Want to share the bed?" he said, exaggeratedly hopeful.

"The couch will be fine."

He sighed. "Goddam, woman, you don't know what you're missing."

She winked at him. "Oh, yes, I do."

six

ALONG with the usual assortment of snow machines and battered pickup trucks, there were half a dozen dog teams staked outside the Roadhouse as Kate drove up the next morning. Mutt leapt off the back of the Jag as they pulled to a halt, and trotted from one team to the next, touching noses with each team's leaders, exchanging sharp, short barks of greeting with the others, not missing anyone, and generally working the crowd in a manner that reminded Kate irresistibly of Ekaterina Shugak working the crowd at an Alaska Federation of Natives meeting. She didn't seem to be interested in much more than touching noses, Kate noticed with mixed feelings of relief and apprehension. Judging by the tracks she'd seen around the woodpile Tuesday morning, tracks the size of salad plates, the timber wolf was still hanging around, hoping, she was grimly convinced, for more than a handout.

A yelp startled her. It wasn't a bark of greeting or a whine for attention, it was a definite yelp for help, and she looked for its source. Around one corner of the building another dog team was anchored almost out of sight. There was another canine yelp and some suppressed snickers of human origin. She took a step forward, the better to see.

The team's lead dog had been restrained by three boys. A fourth had a stick and with it was investigating the dog's behind. The dog yelped a third time. Kate took half a dozen swift noiseless steps and collared the boy with the

stick and the one holding the dog's hind legs apart. Their heads thumped together with a very satisfying sound, so she did it again. The other two boys cut and ran. "Mutt, fetch!" Mutt bounded forward and knocked the third boy over with a powerful shoulder. She left him to nip at the rapidly retreating behind of the fourth. The third boy, still rolling, bounced off the side of the Roadhouse, jumped to his feet and streaked off.

"All right," Kate said, "now just who do we have here?" She twisted them around to see. Bewildered and blubbering, neither was much above ten years old. "Ah. Amos Totemoff. I'll be sure, next time I see Demetri to tell him I saw his son, and I'll be sure to tell him what I saw his son doing, too." She looked at the other boy and said musingly, "Larry? Lyndon? Leonard, that's it, Leonard Kvasnikof. Stop that bawling this instant." Her raspy voice cracked like a broken whip. Both boys froze into immobility, feet dangling some inches above the ground. "Who were those other two boys?" Neither spoke, and she wound her fists tighter in their collars and gave them a shake. "Who were they?"

Still no answer. "Okay," Kate said, easing her grip so that their toes could touch the ground, "I wouldn't give two cents for a boy who ratted on a friend anyway. But get this and get it good. I catch either one of you mistreating a dog, or any other animal anywhere in the Park ever again, I'll blister both your butts until you have to eat standing up for a month. And then I'll tell your dads, and you may never eat sitting down again. Got that?" She banged their heads together a third time, for insurance, and let them fall into two heaps, faces dazed, too stunned to cry.

Kate lifted the leader's tail and didn't see any blood. She gave him a reassuring thump, led the team around to the front of the building with the rest of the sleds, and reset the anchors.

Inside, the Roadhouse was filled to overflowing with what at first seemed one large, amorphous crowd, but

which upon closer inspection resolved into three distinct groups. In one corner a man read from a Bible, hand upraised to heaven, forefinger pointing the one way. A group of six people in folding chairs lined up before him in two orderly rows.

"Pastor Bill," Kate said, nodding.

"Good to see you, Kate," the pastor said, and dropped his forefinger to shake her hand. Without missing a beat the forefinger resumed its upright position, and the sermon continued. "And when the children of Israel saw it, they said one to another, It is—"

"Beer!" a man yelled from the group of tables shoved together in another corner. Behind the bar Bernie nodded and set up another round. Kate recognized them as mushers and, standing on tiptoe and craning her neck, saw that they were hunched over a topographical map of interior Alaska, covering all the Park from Canada to the Alaska Railroad and Prince William Sound to Fairbanks. One of the mushers looked up, caught her eye and waved. "Hey, Kate."

"Hey, Mandy. What's up?"

The stocky woman, eyes crinkled at the corners from squinting long distances into setting Arctic suns, gestured at the map. "Working out a route for the Kanuyaq 500."

"The Kanuyaq 500? What's that?"

"A new race we're organizing. What?" She turned back. "No, no, no, not that way. You want the route to go right through the Valley of Death and straight up Angqaq Peak? It won't be much of a race if we get all the dogs killed in an avalanche." Mandy's smile faded. "Jesus, just think what 'Wide World of Sports' would have to say if we ran a bunch of dogs off Carlson Icefall."

"Compared to what they might say if you only ran the mushers off it," Kate heard a loud voice comment from the next group over, and there was a low laugh, quickly stifled when Mandy glared.

Kate followed the sound of that voice to a group of

matrons sitting around a square piece of cloth. One woman sensed her presence and looked up. "Kate!"

"Hello, Helen." She nodded around the circle. "Kathy, Joyce, Darlene, Gladys, Shirley. How are you all?"

Shirley waved a thick white porcelain mug in her direction. Identical mugs sat on the floor next to each chair. "Pull up a seat! Want an Irish coffee? Bernie!" she bellowed. "Bring Kate an Irish coffee!"

"No," Kate said quickly, shaking her head at Bernie. "I can't, Shirley, I'm driving."

"No? Well, hell, Kate." Shirley, a redhead with pale, freckled skin, grinned up at her. "If you aren't going to drink, sit down and sew a patch or two."

"Love to," Kate said, "if you're sure you're up to it. I remember last time I sewed the quilt to my jeans and it took you guys fifteen minutes to cut me loose."

"You were a little nervous," Gladys, a plump, motherly woman with dark hair, allowed.

"All those seam rippers that close to my lap, you bet I was nervous," Kate retorted. The circle of women cackled reminiscently. Kate looked at the cloth, trying to identify the pattern. "What do you call this one?"

"The wedding ring." Darlene winked at her. "Play your cards right, Kate, and we'll give it to you for a wedding present."

"I have to get married first?"

"Yup." All five graying heads nodded solemnly.

"Then forget it. I can't get married. Who would Chopper Jim and Dandy Mike have to chase if I did?"

Delighted, the circle cackled again. Kate waved a general good-bye and stepped to the long bar at the back of the room. Next to her Mutt reared up, both paws on the bar, panting slightly around an anticipatory tongue. Bernie reached across and scratched behind her ears. "Hey, Mutt, how are you, girl? What'll it be, the usual?"

Mutt yipped once. Bernie pulled a package of beef jerky off a stand and ripped it open. Mutt received it delicately

between her teeth and returned to ground level.

Bernie looked at Kate. "Hi, Kate. Coke?"

She nodded. "Thanks."

He reached for a nozzle and a glass. "What brings you into town? Kind of early for you; you usually don't run your snow machine during breakup." He grinned at her. "Earthquake weather."

She rapped her knuckles on the scarred surface of the wooden bar. "Bite your tongue."

"Yeah, well, I missed the last big one."

"If you're lucky you'll miss the next one, too," Kate said, a little grimly.

He set the glass on a napkin and slid both over in front of her. Leaning forward on folded arms, he regarded her with a slight smile. He had high cheekbones and a higher forehead accentuated by the hair skinned back from both in a neat ponytail as long as Kate's. His eyes were brown and deeply set, their expression always tranquil. Bernie projected a kind of monastic serenity, which, with a wife and seven children in the rambling house fifty yards from the Roadhouse, was a neat trick, now that Kate thought of it. "How's Enid?"

"Fine."

"And the kids?"

"We got the Class C state championship this year, did you hear?" he said proudly.

"No, Bernie," Kate said in a patient voice, "I meant *your* kids. Your very own children. Of Enid born," she elaborated when he looked confused. "Remember? Your wife? My cousin?"

His face cleared. "Oh yeah. Them. They're fine." He thought. "Sammy'll be old enough to try out for the junior varsity team next year."

"How nice for you both," Kate murmured. "When do the playoffs begin?"

"Thursday afternoon," he said, his face reanimating.

"Have we got a shot?"

"We always have a shot," he said loftily. "I been drilling the starting five in free throws since September, Eknaty Kvasnikof's shooting seventy-two percent and the other four aren't much below sixty." He waggled a finger at her. "And remember—"

"Free throws win ball games," she chanted with him and laughed. "Free throws win ball games," was Bernie's mantra. She took a sip. "Where were you, Saturday before last?"

"When McAniff was on his spree?" She nodded. "Right here, along with about half the town, which was probably a good thing."

"Typical Saturday morning," she suggested, and he nodded agreement.

"Crazy bastard," he said. "He must have known he'd get caught."

"I think he was looking forward to it."

Bernie shook his head. "Crazy *sick* bastard. I'll bet he can't wait for the trial so he can tell us how he planned it all."

Kate's generous mouth turned down at the corners. "Safe bet. Jack Morgan told me his lawyers are planning on pleading guilty by reason of insanity."

"So?"

She set her glass down. "They're saying he's insane because he had a bad case of cabin fever brought on by eating too much junk food."

He stared at her for a long moment. "Right," he said at last. "I'll remember to pig out on caramel corn first, the next time I want to shoot somebody and get away with it."

"Bernie," she said and paused. What could he know about any of it, serving up beer and wine coolers across a bar twenty-seven miles downriver from Niniltna and the events of that terrible day? "Did you know him?" she asked finally.

"McAniff?"

"Umm."

He shrugged. "Not really. I knew him enough to call him by name."

"So he came in here?"

"Once in a while."

"What'd he drink?"

"Beer, mostly. Beer and a shot, every now and then."

"What was he like?"

"Quiet. Kept to himself."

"Did he run a tab?"

"Always paid in cash." He eyed her, curious. "Why all the questions? You caught him, right? He's in jail, they got the rifle, they got the bodies, he's bragging he did it on every TV and radio station that'll hold a mike still long enough for him to talk into it. Why do you want to know about him?"

Why did she? Perhaps because she couldn't forget the sight of McAniff lying on the hard-packed snow, weeping when he found himself drooling blood. Maybe she just wanted confirmation of her own actions, validation of the rightness of her cause. "He asked me if I had anything to eat," she said. "Like he was a neighbor who'd been out doing a little hunting and had lost track of time and missed his lunch."

"He would have killed you," Bernie said. "I mean, he had the rifle up and everything, right?"

"Yes."

"You stopped him."

"Mutt did." Hearing her name, Mutt looked up and beat her tail on the floor, chewing on the last piece of jerky.

"Whatever. Somebody had to, Kate." He shot her a keen glance. "You're not going all soft on me, are you? He had to be stopped, Kate. It's a shame—" He stopped and began studiously polishing a glass.

"I know, it's a shame I didn't shoot him when I had the chance." She blew out a sigh and with a firm hand directed the conversation into a useful channel. "Lisa Getty was one of the victims."

"Yeah. I'll miss her."

She felt a pang of dismay. "Bernie. Not you, too."

"Well, she did dress up the place." He pursed his lips as if about to whistle. "Did she ever. Just walking in, she dressed up the place. She brought in the business, too. I think half the guys who came here, came here hoping Lisa'd be here that night. Wherever the biggest bunch of men were in the room, you could bet Lisa'd be in the middle of them. What a honeypot."

Kate rolled her eyes, and Bernie grinned, his monastic restraint suspended for the duration. "Well, she was."

"Lisa interested in anybody in particular?" Kate said, eyes on her glass.

Bernie snorted. "Sure. Every guy she ever laid eyes on. Old men, middle-aged men, boys." He reflected. "I think half the team had the hots for her. Eknaty Kvasnikof did odd jobs for the Getty sisters. Since the massacre he's been dragging around like a whipped pup." His face darkened. "Better not screw with his free-throw average or I'll dig the bitch up and burn her at the stake. And I'll get Pastor Bill to exorcise the remains."

Kate took another sip. "Lisa interested in anyone in particular lately?"

There was a long pause, and she looked up to see Bernie watching her. "Why?"

"Bobby tells me half the Park's gone into mourning for Lisa Getty."

"The male half, sure enough," Bernie agreed. "The female half, that's another story. They're thinking of catering a party." He reached for a glass and began polishing it with a rag, a thoughtful expression on his face. "You grew up with Lisa, didn't you?"

She nodded. "And Lottie."

"Lottie." He shook his head. "They ruined a hell of a man when they cut the balls off her."

"Bernie."

"Sorry," Bernie said, not at all penitently. He set the glass aside and began polishing the bar instead. "But it'd be hard to find two people less alike than the Getty sisters."

"They were both blond and blue-eyed," Kate offered. It was a weak observation and she knew it, but some atavistic impulse of loyalty triggered by a shared childhood, and perhaps a smattering of lingering guilt leftover from her intrusion into Lottie's grief, made her offer up what defense she could. Defense from what? she wondered then. She was thirty years old, almost thirty-one. Surely by now she had rid herself of the us-versus-them complex every Alaskan inevitably developed between we-who-were-born-here and them-who-weren't. She studied her glass. "So Lisa was in here a lot."

"Three, four times a week."

"Always at the center of a group."

Bernie's voice retreated once again into caution. "Well, now, I wouldn't say *always.*"

Not for the first time Kate cursed Bernie's rigid standards. Bernie figured your life was your business and what you did with it the same, including alcoholism, doping, adultery—anything he regarded as a victimless crime. He didn't care what you did as long as you weren't hurting anyone else by your actions. He didn't have to talk about it, either, and he wouldn't. Kate decided she was going to have to prime the pump. "I was out to their place yesterday morning, to talk to Lottie, see if there was anything I could do." Kate drew a circle on the bar with the bottom of her glass. "I wandered around outside afterward." She raised her eyes. "I found a greenhouse behind their barn."

"Did you?" The rag paused in its lazy swipe down the scarred wood of the bar.

"I did." Kate put down her glass with deliberate care. "Bernie, was Lisa dealing dope?"

Bernie looked at her with a meditative expression. A jingle of what sounded like bells came from the back

room, and there was a shout of laughter from the quilt-ing bee, laughter that sounded almost relieved, as if the quilters were happy to discover they still knew how. The pastor paused in his peroration, and the congregation bent its collective head in prayer. "We planning on mushing five hundred miles or five thousand?" Kate heard Mandy say with exasperation. "I know I said we should make it a challenge, but that doesn't mean we should break trail for Toronto."

Bernie shook out the bar rag and folded it with deliber-ate movements. "She's dead, Bernie," Kate told him. "It can't hurt her to talk about it now."

"That's right," Bernie agreed, draping the folded rag over a faucet with elaborate care. "She is dead, so what can it possibly matter now?"

Bernie's usually calm brown eyes could be piercing-ly acute on occasion, Kate discovered. "It does matter, Bernie."

"Why?"

"It matters," she repeated. "I need to know. Was Lisa Getty dealing dope?"

The minister said "Amen," in a voice that echoed around the bar. Amid the resulting momentary silence, he looked over at Bernie. "Coffee all around?"

"Coming right up, Pastor Bill." Bernie loaded a tray with seven mugs, sugar, cream and a pot of coffee and took it over to a table near the congregation. He stood for a few moments, exchanging greetings in his usual quiet, amicable manner. The parishioners rearranged their pews around a table and Bernie poured out the coffee. After a few more words, Bernie returned to the bar. "I suppose if I asked why it matters, you wouldn't tell me."

"Don't ask."

"Hmm." Sam Dementieff, a grizzled old man moving slow but spry, exchanged a gruff greeting with Kate, ordered a shot and a beer and took himself off into a corner, to sit at a table alone and stare broodingly and

forbiddingly at nothing in particular that Kate could see. "Okay," Bernie said finally. Kate swiveled around to look at him. "Yes. She was dealing dope."

"You catch her at it?"

He shook his head. "She was too slick for that. I don't think anything ever changed hands in here. She knew enough not to shit in my nest, but she made plenty of trips outside."

"Are you sure of the reason?"

The laugh lines at the corners of Bernie's eyes deepened. "I don't think even Lisa had that many guys on a string at the same time."

"How many?"

He shrugged. "Depended on the night, the crowd, I imagine her supply. A dozen, two. Never stayed out more than a few minutes."

"She keep it stashed outside somewhere?"

"Must have."

"You ever look for it?"

"Once or twice. Never found it, though. She was good." Bernie gave Kate a faint smile. "In more ways than one."

Kate looked at him, at the reminiscent quirk at the corner of his mouth, and sighed inwardly. To simplify things, she might as well assume that every man in the Park between puberty and senility had slept with Lisa Getty. And suspect every woman of murder, and thought of Enid, a funny, fiery brunette with a broad smile and broader hips and a temper that could smelt steel. "What did you hear about her as a dealer? Was it good dope? Did you get what you paid for?"

"I never heard any complaints."

"Nobody looking for her with a mad-on?"

"Not with a mad-on, no," Bernie said and grinned at Kate's expression.

Someone called for another round at the end of the bar and he strolled off to fill it. Kate turned, leaning her elbows on the upholstered edge, and surveyed the

room. To all outward appearances, it was a Wednesday like any other at Bernie's Roadhouse. The crowd was nothing out of the usual: mushers, quilters, parishioners, serious drinkers who bellied up to the bar at 8:01 A.M., homesteaders there to enjoy Bernie's flush toilet, Park rats looking for company, fishermen like Sam Dementieff planning this year's assault on the first run of salmon. True, the laughter sounded a trifle forced, the conversation a bit stilted, and the attention seemed unnaturally fixed. The whole scene felt unreal, as if the roomful of people had joined together in an unspoken decision to repudiate the horrible reality of the events of the Saturday before last. There was a sense of gritted teeth behind the grins, a shaken but solid persistence in the good cheer, a determined normality in action. In summer, their ranks swollen double by the influx of fishermen, the population of Niniltna, including all the outlying cabins and homesteads and mines and fishing sites, usually ran at sixteen hundred-plus. In winter, the numbers dropped back down to less than eight hundred, eight hundred people bound together in the common struggle to survive the cold and the dark, and to stay sane while they did. Nine of their neighbors were now dead, and laid to rest beneath the scrub spruce and spindly birches in the small, fenced cemetery on the hill in back of the town. These people were gathered together today to seek and receive comfort from the presence of their friends, to present a united front against the madness forced upon them from inside.

In the Alaskan bush it is a long summer day's journey into that winter night, but the night is longer still, and very dark, and very, very cold. Buried deep in the consciousness of every Park rat present was the knowledge that the seeds of madness lay within each of them, seeds which, bred on darkness and suckled on the frigid milk of a seemingly endless winter, were all too capable of burgeoning forth into the blood-red blooms of paranoia and dementia. The knowledge of the possibility was there, in the eyes of

everyone present. The knowledge, as well as the determination to defeat it. It was a good effort, Kate thought, and raised her glass in silent tribute.

The door burst open and there flooded in what seemed like a mob of people, which after a few noisy, confused moments settled into half a dozen men and two women, dressed in down jumpsuits and parkas and bunny boots, bulky garments that made them look bear-size. Their faces were red with sunburn, none of them looked as if they'd had a bath in memory of man, and as they came closer Kate's nose told her they smelled the same way. Climbers. You could always tell, if not by the smell, then by the exhausted exaltation on their faces.

This shouting, laughing, odoriferous human wave surged across the floor and broke against the bar. "You Bernie?" the tallest, burliest and smelliest man demanded.

"So they tell me," Bernie drawled.

The stranger drew himself up to his full height. "I'm Doug, and I just climbed Angqaq Peak." A cheer rose up. "We all did," he said, looking around at his companions.

"You make the summit?"

"Damn straight we made the summit!" Doug whooped, and for a minute the rafters rung with the deep-throated yells of the climbers. When the noise died down, Doug turned back to Bernie. "George Perry told us that before we're confirmed as bona fide Big Bumpers we had to stop in here and have a drink called a Middle Finger."

"That's right," Bernie said, "you do."

"Well?" Doug looked around him. "Eight Middle Fingers, straight up, barkeep."

"And keep 'em coming!" one of the other climbers called, and his friends whooped and beat him on the back.

Bernie waited for the hubbub to die down before saying, "Take off your gloves."

"What?"

"Take off your gloves," Bernie repeated.

The climbers exchanged mystified glances but complied. They began to be uneasily aware of the interest they were generating, the broad general grin that sprawled across the expectant face of everyone in the room.

"All right," Bernie said again. "One at a time, step up, hold up your hands and spread your fingers." He reached beneath the bar and produced eight shot glasses. Turning, he took down a fifth of some clear liquor sitting in the absolute center of the middle shelf, with the rest of the bottles drawn respectfully off to the right and left, and set it down on the counter next to the shot glasses.

Doug looked at the bottle. "What the hell?" Beneath its sunburn his face lost color.

"Along about 1949," Bernie said, his voice pitched to carry, "some surveyors made a trip up Angqaq to see what they could see. They didn't have a clue about climbing a mountain like the Big Bump, they didn't have much equipment or anything in the way of survival gear, and what happened was what you might expect: They got caught in a blizzard and two of them froze to death. The third survived in spite of a case of serious frostbite, which cost him three fingers off his left hand." He paused and surveyed the sobering faces of the climbers. "Before I built the Roadhouse, a guy by the name of Sneaky Pete had a kind of trading post here, and the surveyor made it back this far and collapsed on his front doorstep. Pete took off the guy's fingers, and he decided, as a lesson to future climbers, that he ought to commemorate the cost of this guy's survival. He dropped the guy's middle finger into a bottle of Everclear. From that day forward it has been required of every climber who successfully makes the summit of Big Bump, *with all their fingers intact,* to toss back a shot of Middle Finger and toast to the memory of those who don't come back, or don't come back whole."

Doug's face was a sight to behold, but he was game. He thrust out his jaw and held up his hands. "One," Bernie said, pointing to Doug's right pinkie finger, "two," pointing to his right ring finger, "three," pointing to his right middle finger, and so on. By Doug's left thumb the entire bar was chanting along, "six, seven, eight, nine, ten!"

There was an electric silence. Bernie uncapped the bottle in which the surveyor's finger washed gently back and forth. Bernie had changed the mix to Jose Cuervo Gold, and after forty-plus years of pickling, the wrinkled skin of the suprisingly well-preserved finger looked as if it had been seasoned with saffron. It still sported a fingernail, Kate noted, and, if she were not mistaken, what might have been a hangnail.

Bernie poured out a shot and waited. Doug took a deep breath, threw back his shoulders, no doubt gave a fleeting thought to the sterilizing effects of eighty-proof alcohol, and in one quick movement raised the shot glass and tossed it off.

The bar thundered with cheers and applause. There was only a slight hesitation before the next climber stepped willingly if unenthusiastically forward, held up her hands, suffered the count and choked back a straight shot of Middle Finger. Each of the climbers followed, and each performance was counted down by the bar in a body, witnessed with bated breath, and cheered with fervor.

The ceremony concluded, people crowded forward to treat the newly inducted Big Bumpers to the Middle Finger chaser of their choice, and the climbers began peeling off their down outerwear with a view to settling in for the afternoon, and perhaps the night.

She'd missed his entrance in the pandemonium following the climber's entrance, so she started when he spoke right next to her. "Kate. How are you?"

Mutt lifted her lip in a perfunctory baring of teeth, not bothering to growl, and Kate turned to see a man with a stiff red face and stiffer red hair about a quarter of an inch

long all over his head. His sharp brown eyes looked less merry than usual, and his stubborn chin jutted out with less than its usual arrogance. His left arm was in a sling.

"Mac," she said, nodding at him.

"I hear you got him," Mac said.

Kate nodded again. She didn't want to talk about it, and she hoped Mac didn't either.

"You should have shot him when you had the chance."

Evidently he did. "So I've been told," she said wearily. "About ten times. Look, Mac, I don't—"

"You don't want to talk about it, fine, you don't have to," he interrupted her. "Just let me say this." He gave her a twisted smile. "When I ran off into the trees with that nut blazing away at my back, my arm bleeding a road map in the snow, I was sure he was following me. I was sure he wasn't going to stop until he got me. His eyes—" Mac halted, and for the first time in Kate's memory he seemed to be at a loss for words. "Well, you saw his eyes. From what I hear, most of the folks he shot at that day didn't get away. I was lucky, but I didn't know that." Bernie set an open Heineken in front of him, and he paused for a long pull. Wiping his mouth, he set the bottle down and regarded it. "I hid out in the woods all night. Every time I heard an owl hoot, I thought it was him. Every time a tree creaked, or the wind blew, or the ice cracked, I thought it was him. I was cold and wet and hungry and tired, but I stayed in the woods. I didn't have any food, or a tent, I wasn't even wearing boots. I was pretty sure I'd heard his snow machine drive away, but I stayed in those goddam woods. I stayed in those goddam woods all that night, all the next day and all the next night, too. If I hadn't seen Chopper Jim land at the mine the next morning, I might still be there. I swear, when Jim told me that you'd caught him, I felt someone reach around and pull the target off my back."

Mac drained his beer and set it down on the bar with a final ring of glass on wood. "I owe you, Kate."

"I didn't save your life, Mac. You did."

"Yeah. But you gave me back my sanity. If you hadn't caught that guy, I'd never have felt safe again." He stretched out a hand, and befuddled, she took it. His grip was strong. "Thanks, Kate."

"You're welcome," she said automatically. A puzzled frown between her brows, she watched his stocky figure thread its way through the crowd and out the door.

"What'd he want?" Bernie's voice asked.

She turned. "Nothing."

Bernie grunted, conveying boundless skepticism in that one sound. "If you say so."

There was a burst of laughter and applause from behind a closed door. "Who is that in the back room, anyway?" Kate asked, glad of a change of subject. "Sounds like they're having some fun now."

"Bunch of belly dancers," Bernie said.

Kate held both hands up, palms out. "Okay, none of my business. Sorry I asked."

"No, really, they rent the back room the first Wednesday of every month to practice."

"Of course they do," Kate said and smiled at Bernie. One must humor those less fortunately endowed than oneself in their degree of sanity.

A small, slight man with Asian features elbowed his way through the crowd. He didn't look like a climber—he wasn't wearing enough clothes—and he didn't smell like a fisherman. It was too late for caribou and too early for black bear. The bump of satiable curiosity that had caused Kate to be an investigator in the first place was roused. She watched him out of the corner of one eye. His look was appraising, his movements furtive. He walked as if he should be wearing a long raincoat, with pockets sewn to the lining filled with stolen watches and dirty postcards.

When he spoke to Bernie, his English was American. "Hi there. Got any draft?"

Bernie shook his head. "Sorry."

"What flavor?" Bernie indicated the row of bottles and cans lining the back of the bar. "Oh. Okay. I'll have a Michelob."

"Coming right up."

He tossed a one-hundred-dollar bill down on the bar and looked around. "Nice place," he observed to Kate.

"We like it," she said, eyeing the bill. "Your first time in the Park?"

He smiled. "First time in Alaska." Bernie set a bottle and a glass on a napkin in front of him. "Can I buy you a drink?"

"Sure," Kate said, and Bernie nodded and went away with the bill. "Where you from?"

"Honolulu." He drank thirstily straight from the bottle.

Kate smiled. "You're a ways from home. What brings you to the Park?"

He shrugged. Bernie came back with his change and Kate's Coke. "Business."

"Oh. Thanks." She raised her glass in the newcomer's direction, turning her shoulder slightly to Bernie. He drifted down to the other end of the bar. She drank. "What kind of business?"

"Import-export," he said. "And you?"

"Oh, I homestead about twenty-five miles from here. I'm Kate Shugak, by the way. And you?"

He took her hand. "Johnny Wu. Live here year round, do you? How long?"

"I was born here."

"Really. That's interesting."

"How about you? How long have you lived in Hawaii?"

"Maybe you can help me," he replied, either not hearing or ignoring her question. "I'm looking for someone."

"Well, I know pretty much everyone in the Park. Who do you want?"

"It's a woman, name of Lisa Getty."

Kate felt a frisson of awareness run up her spine. "Lisa Getty?"

"Yes. A . . . mutual friend gave me her name, said she was the best guide in the Park."

"Lisa Getty is dead," Kate said bluntly. The smile was wiped from his face, and she congratulated herself inwardly that her cop's eye was still in. "Didn't you hear about the massacre?"

"Massacre? What massacre?"

"A week, week and a half ago. Some Park rat went nuts with a 30.06. Lisa Getty was one of the victims."

"Jesus," Wu said.

"Sorry to have to be the one to tell you," she said. "You know Lisa yourself?"

"No," he muttered, his face pale, grabbing his beer. "I never met her personally." He tilted the bottle up and gulped thirstily.

"I do some guiding myself, in season," Kate offered. "Maybe we could work something out. You didn't say what you were after—bear? Did Lisa organize you a permit?"

He smiled, a sick smile, and set the empty bottle down. "Thanks anyway. This whole thing is pretty— pretty shocking. I think I'll—" He got off his bar stool without finishing his sentence and picked up his bag.

"You need a place to stay?"

He shook his head and went to the door. Kate watched him go, a thoughtful expression on her face, and turned back to the bar to find Bernie watching her. "What?" she said.

"Nothing."

"You hear all that?"

"Most of it."

"Seen him around before?"

Bernie was silent for a moment. Finally he said, "Not him, no."

She paused in the act of raising her glass and stared at him over the rim. His expression was bland. "Right," she said finally and drank. "See you."

"I wonder where you're going."

Her eyes narrowed. "No, you don't."

She stood up just as the door to the back room opened and, to Kate's dumb amazement, a group of belly dancers came out. One of them was in full regalia, all diaphanous gauze and jingling gold coins, laughing eyes above a sheer veil. A second dancer in bikini bra and jeans struck a tambourine, a third in shorts and a tank top blew on a flute, and a collective whoop went up around the house.

Kate looked at Bernie, open-mouthed. He grinned at her expression and gave a deprecating shrug. The dancers began to shimmy, and the congregation deserted their pastor and the mushers their map to join the climbers and the other miscellaneous drinkers in a shouting circle that beat time with their hands. Only the quilters stayed where they were, plying needles and tongues with equal intensity. Kate shook her head in disbelief and made for the door, passing near the quilters on her way out.

"So did she divorce him?"

"Heavens no, dear. She wanted one. He drowned before he could give it to her."

"They do say . . ."

"What?"

"What do they say?"

"What, Darlene?"

"Well," Darlene said, leaning forward and dropping her voice, "you know they found him floating at the bottom of the ramp . . ."

"Yes, yes?"

"Someone said they saw her down there, too, that morning."

"No!"

The door closed behind Kate. Blinking as her eyes adjusted from the gloom of the bar to the bright light of the afternoon, she saw Leonard and Amos sitting together at the top of the stairs, playing scissors-paper-stone. As she watched, Leonard lost and took a wallop on his upper arm

from Amos's clenched fist. Kate took careful aim with one booted foot and kicked them both down the stairs.

She climbed on the Super Jag as they were picking themselves up out of the snow, motioned Mutt up behind her, and left.

Lisa Getty's bowpicker was racked up above the high tide mark, side by side with thirty others, all waiting for the ice to go out of the river before their hulls could hit water.

It was a thirty-two foot bowpicker with a bare, stainless-steel reel in the bow and a square, squatty cabin that filled up the stern. Between them was the hold, covered over in wooden deck planking. In appearance it had much in common with the Getty's homestead, as it was messy but in good repair, and clean if not neat. There were old tracks of a very small boot in the thin layer of crusting snow on deck. Kate climbed aboard and began to pull up the deck planks—long, one-by-twelve-by-twelves laid side by side across the inner lip of the holding tank. Mutt wagged her tail encouragingly from her comfortable seat on the mat in front of the cabin door.

It was noon, and the sun was shining, and Kate was sweating before she had enough planks up to climb down into the hold.

She surfaced some twenty minutes later, puzzled. The hold was empty, without a net, corkline, leadline or buoy to be found. She'd even pried up the floorboards and checked the bilge. Bone dry from a winter in dry dock, it, too, was empty, from stem to stern.

She replaced the floorboards and straightened, groaning a little when her back creaked in protest. "It has to be here if it's anywhere," she told Mutt.

"Woof," Mutt agreed without moving.

"You're a big help." Putting both hands flat on the lip of the hatch, Kate lifted herself up and over into a sitting position at the hatch's edge. Her legs dangling in the hold, she turned her face up into the sun, closed

her eyes and thought out loud. "When we were kids, Lisa never left all her stuff in one place. She had toys stashed in hidey-holes all over—in the tent we pitched up the hill in back of her parents' house, in the tree house we built in the cottonwood in Big Monkey-Land down on Humpy Creek, on her dad's boat, in her uncle's cache, in her locker at school, hell, in her desk at school. She spread things around; she always did. If she was growing dope at home, ten to one she was selling what she poached out of somewhere else. Besides, at home there was Lottie, who I know for a fact disapproves of flying and shooting the same day, never mind shooting at something on the endangered species list. She'd probably have turned Lisa in herself, if she'd caught her at it." Kate paused. "If she'd caught her at it." She looked down at Mutt, who stared solemnly back. "Anyway, the boat was in town and closer to hand. Closer to the airstrip, for that matter, and to planes headed out of the Park."

Mutt rested her chin on her forepaws and prepared to be patient. Somewhere down the beach a couple of sea gulls raised their voices in raucous dispute, a crow cawed mockingly from overhead, a slight breeze rustled through the alders crowded against the high water mark. That same breeze lifted the wisps of hair escaping from Kate's single braid. A hammer beat rhythmically against a metal surface, paused, resumed. The ice in the river shifted and cracked over the gray, thickly silted water beneath. As the brims of ice-cap glaciers dissolved in the warmer temperatures of the ever-increasing daylight, as the winter's snowpack melted, the runoff filled the streams and creeks and poured into tributaries and from them into the Kanuyaq. Daily, the volume and speed of the river increased, and would soon peel the caked, cracked rind of winter from the river's surface, sweeping it downstream, into Prince William Sound and the Gulf of Alaska and out to

sea, leaving behind a new, swelling, rushing skin of pearlescent gray, a living, gleaming, 250-mile ribbon adorning the awakening landscape of the Park, fecund with the promise of spring and the first run of salmon.

There is nothing tentative or uncertain about the coming of spring in the Arctic; it does not creep in unannounced. It marches in at the head of an invading army, all flags flying, brass brand playing, soldiers at present arms and knee-deep in ticker tape and cheers. Suddenly and with all her heart Kate longed to be home, back at the homestead, to participate in the rambunctious toss and jostle as breakup elbowed its way into the Park. The trunks of the birches were dark with the subdermal flow of sap; the scab of ice on Silver Creek at the foot of the ravine in back of her cabin was breaking off in larger and larger chunks; the Quilak Mountains were shrugging out of their winter coats and striding bare-breasted into spring. Away from it for twenty-four hours, she missed home with an aching intensity that brought a rueful smile of self-acknowledgment.

"Maybe Jack's right and I am just a hermit at heart," she told Mutt. She should have gotten on with her search. Instead she stretched out on the deck, burrowed her head into Mutt's furry side and let the sun pour down over her.

A half hour later a sudden chill woke her from a light doze. She shivered and sat up, blinking. A tumble of cumulus clouds elbowed its way up out of the southeast horizon, jostling for position between Kate and the sun. "See that," she said, slapping Mutt affectionately on the flank, "a cloud comes over the sunlit arch, a wind comes off a frozen peak and you're all at once back in the middle of March. The poet was right."

She rose to her feet and stretched her arms over her head, yawning. "I suppose I should check the cabin, although I can't imagine Lisa'd be dumb enough to leave anything right where some drunked-up teenager

vandalizing dry-docked boats on a dare could stumble
across it. But if Wu's in the Park, the stuff's got to be
somewhere."

Still half-asleep, she grappled with the hasp, upon
which Lisa had not bothered herself to install a pad-
lock. Sliding the little door to one side, she took a step
forward, tripped over an unstowed boat hook and fell
headlong through the cabin door.

Which was a very good thing, since the shooter
hunkered down in the clump of alders at the head of
the beach chose that very moment to squeeze off a shot
in her direction.

The sharp report echoed across the expanse of sand
and gravel and ice. Something nudged the side of Kate's
head, and something warm began to flow down over the
right side of her face and drip off her chin. She fell
hard and loose, hitting her shoulder against the edge
of the bunk built into the back of the cabin. Her
head started to hurt. She raised a hand and touched
it, and saw that the liquid was blood. All the strength
seemed to go out of her limbs and a smothering
wave of darkness rose up and overwhelmed her.

When she woke, her eyelids seemed stuck together. It took
her a moment to get them open. Her cheek was pressed
against a hard surface and seemed also to be stuck there.
Someone was rubbing a rough, wet washcloth over her
face. A dog whined, and she stirred. She knew that whine,
and memory returned in a sudden rush. "Mutt?" Her hands
fumbled around for purchase and she pushed up. The skin
of her cheek pulled off the floor with a sticky sound.

At her side, Mutt whined anxiously. She licked Kate
again.

Her head was pounding. Kate raised a shaky hand and
investigated. Where the bullet had plowed across her temple there was a shallow wound a half-inch wide and two
inches long. Blood must have drained from it into her eyes

and down the right side of her face and into the collar of her shirt. The smell of blood was everywhere, but the area around the wound seemed cleaner than the rest of her. Mutt whined again, her muzzle thrust directly in Kate's face, her yellow eyes round and anxious, and licked her cheek yet again.

" 'S okay," Kate muttered, holding her off, "head wounds always bleed like hell. Get fixed up in a minute. 'S okay, girl, take it easy." With hands seemingly too swollen to perform even the most simple task, she fumbled around in her pockets for a kerchief. It took what felt like forever to find one, and when she did, it took another forever to fold it and bind it around her forehead. Reaching up over the edge of the tiny sink, praying that the water tank wasn't empty, she was rewarded by a thin stream of cool water. She splashed some on her face, a scant handful at a time. Blinking her eyes clear, she inched over to the door and peered up over the sill.

Outside, the sky had cleared again, and the sun seemed to have dropped like a golden stone into a pale blue pond, cumulus ripples spreading out to the very edge of the horizon. Kate blinked again and realized it was coming up on sunset. She must have been out for hours. She could see nothing out of the ordinary, hear nothing out of the ordinary. No one had come running, so the hammerer had not heard the shot and was long since gone. From the town up the bank and beyond the trees smoke rose from chimneys in peaceful white wisps. Even the gulls were silent.

Leaning back, Kate looked around the cabin and found a knit watch cap of navy blue. With the cap over the end of the boat hook that had tripped her up, she poked them both out the door of the bowpicker's cabin, very slowly. Mutt, still on her feet with her eyes fixed unwaveringly on Kate's face, didn't move.

The cap crept up over the sill, the level of the deck, the railing. Nothing. No sound, no movement, nobody shoot

ing. Kate swung the boat hook back and, swinging it with both hands, threw the cap across the deck into the bow. Still nothing.

The boat hook fell clattering to the deck. Whoever the shooter had been, they were gone now. Kate lay where she was and shook for a while. She felt she'd earned it.

After a moment she remembered there was something she was supposed to do. Groaning, she pulled herself up by the edge of the bunk, raising herself to her feet to begin the search. Hampered by the dimming light, her pounding head, and having to do most of it by touch, nevertheless it didn't take long to find what she was looking for. In the locker mounted on the bulkhead above the bunk, hidden behind the canned goods, she found a creased paper bag with the top folded down. Inside were half a dozen greenish-yellow, wizened-up little bags of what seemed to be dried meat. She put the bag to one side to rummage further. Not for a moment did she believe she had found all there was to find, and proved herself right almost immediately.

She pulled back the mattress and knocked against the sheet of plywood beneath. Lifting the mattress completely out of the bunk, she felt around the edges with inquisitive fingers until she found a line of three small holes sanded smooth at one end. Her fingers slid in and she lifted. In the shallow hollow between engine compartment and mattress bottom, tucked between a clutch of plastic mending needles and a damp, disintegrating cardboard box full of rusting nuts, bolts and nails, she found two sets of walrus tusks with skulls. Forgetting, she whistled, long and low. The sound hurt her ears. One of the sets was trophy-size, with tusks thirty inches long and perfectly matched.

Dizzy, aching, sick as she was, the arrogance of it amazed her. To leave a set of ivory tusks worth a minimum of $3,000 on the black market in the cubby beneath the bunk, to leave half a dozen black bear gall bladders worth anywhere from $600 to $1,000 apiece in Hong

Kong practically out in plain sight in the locker above
that bunk, and all behind a door Lisa hadn't bothered
to lock—a wave of nausea engulfed her. Kate held her
head on with both hands and staggered out to retch over
the side.

Rinsing out her mouth in the sink she searched further
without result, which did surprise her. By this time Jack
Morgan could have accused Lisa Getty of selling mili-
tary secrets to Moammar Qaddafi and Kate would have
believed him without question. She replaced plywood and
mattress and climbed shakily out of the cabin, carrying
the paper bag and the tusks. Looking over the side at
the eight-foot drop to the ground, she swore weakly.
She tossed the bag over, let the tusks down more gently
and somehow managed to maneuver herself to the edge
and over, landing on legs that promptly collapsed. Mutt
jumped down next to her and touched a cold nose to her
cheek.

Kate raised a feeble hand and shoved at her. "I'm all
right, girl, just give me a minute."

One minute passed, another, and still Kate lay there, her
head pounding, her vision swimming, until Mutt set her
teeth in Kate's collar and began to tug.

"Oh, for Christ's sake, all right already," Kate said
wearily. With a tremendous effort she made it to her
knees and had to pause there, retching emptily between
trembling arms braced wide apart. She wobbled to her
feet, leaning up against the bowpicker's hull. When she
remembered how to walk, she picked up the bag and the
tusks, which now seemed to weigh one hundred pounds
each, and staggered out from between the boats and up the
bank to her snow machine.

She never remembered getting the seat locker on the
Jag open. She never remembered whether she went
through the village or around it. She never remembered
the two-mile trip over the rough, rutted, icy track that led
to Bobby's house. If she'd been a fanciful woman she

would have thought that Mutt drove the snow machine, or at least steered it. She did have a clear, painful memory of falling, hard, as if dropped from a great height, on the ramp just two steps shy of Bobby's front door, but those two steps took on the width of the Atlantic Ocean and Kate had gone as far as she could. She was dimly aware of a rough, wet tongue washing her face, of a dog whining anxiously somewhere, of a far-off wish that she could respond, of the bitter knowledge that she could not. Only the smell of blood was clear and definite and wholly undeniable, clinging tenaciously to her nostrils, so strong it was almost a salt taste on her tongue. The sun had set by now, and she began to shiver. She made a tremendous effort and stretched one hand toward the door, managing to move it perhaps six inches before the effort proved too much. In a part of her mind wholly detached from her dilemma, she wondered if she was going to die of exposure, there on Bobby's front porch.

But Bobby heard them, and forever after Kate remembered the sudden shaft of light streaming from his front door to illuminate what felt like her final resting place, the reassuring roar of his deep voice. "Kate! Goddammit, Mutt, move your ass out of the way! Woman, what the fuck have you done to yourself now?"

And then, mercifully, oblivion.

seven

HER eyes opened the next morning promptly at six. She stared up at the steeply pitched roof of a cedar A-frame that after some thought she recognized as Bobby's. Her head ached, but at a distance, as if the pain was happening to someone else. Her arms and legs felt heavy, and when she brought up one hand to push the covers down it was like she was pushing her way through very deep water.

The sheets on the bed felt soft on her bare skin. Someone had undressed her. Shifting against the pillow, she felt something bulky on the right side of her head. Reaching up, she discovered a bandage taped to her temple. It throbbed when she touched it, and she dropped her hand. She became aware of a solid warmth lying next to her. Cautiously, she investigated. It was a body, not her own. She turned her head and met Bobby's eyes, and managed to summon up what felt like a very weak smile. "Some guys'll do anything to get laid."

He waggled his bushy black eyebrows. "If the woman is you, it's worth the effort."

"I bet you say that to all the girls." Her head gave a vicious throb, and she winced, her face paling.

His smile faded. He raised one hand and smoothed her hair back from her face. "How you feeling, woman? Head hurt?"

111

She closed her eyes and thought. "Not much more than if a guy was whanging away at the inside of my skull with a sledgehammer."

"Oh well, then you're definitely recovering."

"What happened?"

"You don't remember?"

She started to shake her head and thought better of it. "I don't even remember how I got here."

Bobby rose up on one elbow. "I don't know how you got here, either. About six last night I heard this thump out on the porch, which was you falling on your face, and I heard Mutt bark. When I opened the door, I thought you were dead. I think Mutt thought so, too; she didn't want to let me touch you. You were a mess, woman, blood all over your face and in your hair and down the front of your jacket and shirt. Looked like you'd been the whole month at Hue, and you smelled that way, too."

"What happened then?"

"I managed to get the goddam wolf quieted down and hauled you inside. I stripped you and washed you off—you tie that bandanna around your head?"

Kate's brow puckered. After a moment she gave a slow, careful nod. "On the boat. When I woke up. I think."

"You must have done it after it stopped bleeding. It didn't stick when I took it off, and it was a lot less bloody than the rest of you."

Kate frowned. "I remember now. Mutt was licking me when I woke up."

"Oh. Good for her. Anyway, I got you cleaned up and into bed. I kept waking you up every hour or so, talking to you, feeding you sweet tea. At first all you could get down was a sip or two, you were cold and clammy, I was an inch away from calling for a medivac. Then, finally, you started to warm up, and I could let you sleep." He looked at her. "I'd like to say right now, you have not been a fun date. Let's not do this again anytime soon."

She gave a ghost of a laugh. "Sorry. I'll try to do better in the future."

His mock severe expression faded. "See you do, woman." He paused and then said, as if the words were forced out of him, "Jesus, but you had me scared." He leaned forward and kissed her lightly. His lips were warm and firm, the hand cupping her face strong and steady, and with a rush of relief and gladness Kate remembered that she was alive and whole and all her parts in working order. Giving an inarticulate murmur of pleasure, she responded, and what might have happened then was anyone's guess, but Mutt, hearing their voices, jumped on the bed and poked her cold, wet nose between them, her yellow eyes wide and expectant, her tail wagging eagerly.

"Goddam, woman," Bobby roared, "can't you teach that goddam wolf some goddam etiquette!"

Someone beat on the door with a large, determined fist and it flew open, banging back against the wall. Kate shut her eyes, wincing. Jack Morgan, looking twice his already extra-large size in parka and bunny boots, stood in the doorway with a hard, anxious look on his face. His gaze found Kate and Bobby instantly.

He looked from Bobby, leaning on one elbow and obviously nude beneath the sheets, to Kate, next to him with the sheets clutched to her breast, also obviously nude. The anxious look faded. Through clenched teeth he enunciated clearly, "Mind telling me just what the hell is going on here?" The effect of icy rage was spoiled somewhat when Mutt bounced over with a joyous bark and reared up, a paw on each shoulder, to lavish his face with a wet and welcoming tongue.

Bobby sat up and waved a magnanimous hand. "Just stealing your woman, Jack old buddy." He tried a leer, but it wasn't up to his usual standard. "And if you'd waited fifteen minutes longer, I might have done it, too."

• • •

Through a mouthful of French toast, Bobby said thickly, "I called him last night after I got you cleaned up."

"I wish you hadn't," Kate muttered.

"Oh no, why should he?" Jack said, sitting very erect and plying his knife and fork with surgical precision. She and Bobby were seated at opposite ends of the table, and Jack was sitting between them, a position he had maintained since Kate had risen, in spite of Mutt's insistence on remaining immediately next to Kate at all times. Kate felt as if she were breathing for three. Bobby, spurred on by who knew what demon of mischief, took every opportunity to touch her, brushing her fingers as he poured her coffee, leaning one hand on her shoulder as he served her breakfast, in passing reaching over to adjust the collar of her newly laundered shirt, all the while with a face like St. Thomas Aquinas, minus the halo.

Jack watched through narrowed eyes but made no comment. Kate, feeling like a particularly tasty bone between two, no, make that three salivating dogs, might have enjoyed herself if she'd been fifteen years younger. At thirty-one, she felt irritated with both men and hoped to get through breakfast without any more blood, in particular hers, being shed than absolutely necessary.

Jack dissected another slice of French toast. "I *told* you to keep your investigation quiet, but noo-ooo, the first thing you do is tell all to the Blabber of the Bush. What, did he put it out on that pirate radio show of his: 'Hey, everybody, somebody killed Lisa Getty, and it wasn't McAniff!' "

"Hey," Bobby said in a hurt voice, pretending wounded feelings he didn't have in hopes of getting another rise out of Jack. He knew perfectly well Jack was spoiling for a fight and would say whatever hurtful thing he could lay tongue to in the process. He also knew that Jack didn't mean a word of it, that he would apologize for it later, and that he would owe Bobby big-time for putting

up with his fouled mood. Bobby smiled to himself and tucked into his breakfast with relish.

"You said you wanted me to handle this," Kate said.

"Yes, I did."

"On the evidence, not one of your better ideas," Bobby observed, and Jack damned him with a single glare.

"Then let me *handle* it," Kate interjected before Jack could start in on Bobby.

"Oh right, you're handling it so well," he retorted, "your second day in you almost get yourself killed."

She shook her head and regretted it. "No, I didn't."

He paused, fork suspended in midair, to give her an incredulous stare. "Of course," he said, very polite. "How silly of me. You weren't shot yesterday. You weren't unconcious for hours on Lisa Getty's boat. You didn't have to crawl on your hands and knees to your snow machine; you didn't fall down unconscious and damn near dead on Bobby's front porch; you don't have a bandage on your head now. In fact, this is all a product of my overactive imagination and I'm going to wake up in Anchorage any minute. Feel free to mix in here anytime," he told Bobby.

"Why should I?" Bobby said, mopping up the last of his syrup. "You're doing fine."

"Look, Kate," Jack said, taking a deep breath and making an obvious grab for some shred of composure, "take it easy today, get your strength back up. Drink a lot, eat a lot, that kind of thing. From what Bobby says, you've lost a lot of blood. I'll take the Jag into Niniltna and nose around, talk to a few people, maybe go up on the Step—"

"No, you won't," Bobby said.

Jack stared at him. "Mind telling me why not?"

"I'm going into town this afternoon. Ekaterina's throwing a potlatch at the gym."

Kate, forgetting her injury, sat up straight. "A potlatch? What for?"

Bobby raised an eyebrow. "To say good-bye to those killed week before last, or so Billy Mike told me when he stopped by. Ekaterina wants everyone to turn out, so he says, and I am not one to spit in the eye of a royal command. So you," he said to Jack, "need to stay and look after Kate."

"Oh," Jack said, adding reluctantly, "okay. I'll stay."

"No," Kate said.

"Why not?"

"For one thing, Nurses Clark and Morgan, I feel fine. For another, I've got an errand to run in Niniltna myself this morning."

Forks clattered to plates. "What? Like hell! You—"

"Woman!" Bobby's roar was back in full force. "You're not going anywhere anytime soon! You just got shot in the goddam head! Not that there was that much there to hit in the first place, but it must've shaken loose what few brains you used to have! You ain't getting on no goddam snow machine and driving *anywhere!*"

She bit down on her last piece of bacon. It crunched satisfyingly between her teeth and almost melted on her tongue, and she closed her eyes reverently.

When she opened her eyes her two men were still yelling at her, with a steady increase in volume. Mutt had risen to her feet and was adding to the general hoopla with short, excited barks. Kate drained her mug, smiled ingratiatingly at Bobby and pitched her voice to cut through the hubbub. "Could I have a refill?"

Bobby dithered and spluttered and finally snapped, "If you're in good enough shape to get on a snow machine, you're in good enough shape to get your own goddam coffee!" He glared at her.

She rose carefully to her feet, pleased to find her legs working, and walked over the stove to refill her cup. Turning, she found both men watching her with varying degrees of frustration. She smiled, a dazzling smile that was two parts mischief to one part seduction and which

she divided impartially between them. Bobby cursed and sailed his fork across the room. After a long, frustrated stare and what was obviously a severe inner struggle, Jack bent his head over his plate and continued eating.

She waited until they finished and, amid thunderous silence, cleared the table, washed the dishes and dried them. Reaching for her parka, she paused in the doorway. "Now," she said, sweetly malicious, "can I trust you two to behave while I'm gone?"

There was a flood of profanity and at least one solid object thudded against the door she hurriedly pulled closed behind her. "Maybe not," she told Mutt, "but boys will be boys."

Mutt gave a reproving growl and turned to stalk stiffly down the drive, disapproval evident in every line of her body. Bloody but unbowed, Kate followed.

She found Johnny Wu the only place he could be, at Auntie Viola's. Her aunt rented out her three spare bedrooms (shared bath, included breakfast) for the highway-robbery amount of $100 a night during those winter months when the Niniltna Lodge was closed. There was nowhere else in town to stay, and you either anted up with a smile or you slept out in the cold. Kate came in just as he was settling his bill, and from the satisfied expression on Aunt Viola's face he had paid in cash. Auntie Viola always preferred cash. She inquired if Mr. Wu cared for a receipt, and beamed to hear that he did not. The cash vanished into a convenient pocket, and she shook Wu's hand heartily and invited his speedy return to her establishment. Over his shoulder she caught sight of Kate in the entryway, stamping slush from her feet. "Kate!" she said with a wide grin. "I didn't know you were in town. This is Mr. Wu, from Outside."

"No, ma'am, I told you before, I'm from Hawaii. How do," he said to Kate, before his eyes widened in

recognition. "Didn't I buy you a drink yesterday at the Roadhouse?"

"You sure did, and I thank you," Kate told him. She gave Auntie Viola, a short, plump woman with a shrewd twinkle in her brown eyes, a quick kiss. "Auntie, could I use your living room? I want to talk to Mr. Wu for a minute."

"Sure, honey, no problem, take your time." Auntie Viola hurried past them to open the door into the living room and ushered them inside. She hesitated in the doorway, flicking at some imaginary dust on the buffet hutch, until Kate assisted her out, closing the door firmly behind her.

Her business with Wu did not take long and they were both very pleased with each other at its conclusion. Kate even gave him a ride to the airstrip on the back of the Jag, turned him over to George Perry personally, helped load his bulging duffel bag into the now reassembled Cessna and waited until it was off the ground.

She gave a final wave as it disappeared into the west. When she lowered her eyes, her gaze became tangled and caught in the stand of trees at the far end of the strip. Their tops clustered together against the almost colorless sky, and their trunks hugged the ground, presenting a stiff, united front. Her good humor faded and her arm dropped to her side. On an impulse she walked forward. All the evidence there was was in the state crime lab in Palmer; she'd seen the inventories and the results of the tests in Jack's files. There was nothing left to look at in the copse that had seen so much blood spilled just ten days before. She told herself all this, and kept walking.

It was another still day, a bare hint of a breeze stirring the air, the sun warm on her back. She entered the woods as she had before, carefully, silently, respectfully, Mutt leading the way. Much of the winter snowpack had melted beneath the onslaught of so many pairs of feet

over the last days, leaving bare, hard ground still frozen beneath the melting slush.

Kate paused and cocked her head. Voices came from somewhere inside the copse. There was a distant, single pop that made her flinch. Low, smothered laughter followed. It was not a pleasant sound. Mutt's ears went up and, her pulse quickening, Kate pushed her way back between the branches.

Kate caught the limb of a birch across her cheek, a spruce elbowed her in the side, a knot of alders tried to trip her up. She fought her way in, ducking and weaving, until she came to the heart of the copse. There she halted, out of breath.

A group of half a dozen women stood in a small circle; surprised faces turned to look at her. A short, plump brunette held a bottle of champagne, the cork out. The rest of the women held glasses filled to the brim with golden bubbling liquid. They gaped at her, until the brunette asked, a little unsteadily, "Come to join in the celebration, Kate?"

"What celebration, Enid?"

Enid gestured with the bottle in a way that made Kate realize that the celebration had begun at the Roadhouse much earlier in the day, perhaps even the previous night. "In memorium." She stumbled over the word, and the rest of the group helped her out—"That's right, in memorium"—although none of them were in much better shape.

Kate looked around and realized they were on the site, or very close to it, where Lisa Getty's body had been found. Incredulous, she asked, "In honor of Lisa Getty?"

Enid snickered. "Hell no." She topped off her glass with an unsteady flourish, emptying the bottle to the last drop. "In honor of Roger McAniff, bless his heart, who shot that fucking bitch and killed her dead. He got it right one time, right, girls?"

"Hear, hear," someone said, and someone else said,

"I'm just sorry it was so quick."

Kate couldn't find a single unfamiliar face. There was Enid, Bernie's wife; there was Sarah, Pete Kvasnikof's wife; there was Susan Moore, Jimmy Bartlett's room-mate-for-life; there was Luz Santos, who had been engaged to Chuck Moonin; there was Betty Sue Brady, Lee's widow; and there was Denise Smithson, whose husband Phil had worked as Lisa's deckhand and then got off the boat in Cordova and got on a plane to Anchorage and never come back. It was a fairly representative cross-section of the Park—tall and short, fair and dark, thin and plump, old and young—with nothing in common but their concentrated hatred of Lisa Getty. "To McAniff!" Enid said, her glass held high, and "To McAniff!" the other women responded. They drank deeply, and when the glasses were drained to the last drop, they threw them against the trunk of a large fir, to shatter and fall to the ground in a glittering, broken shower that mingled with the half-ice, half-slush layer of snow until it was impossible to tell where the shards of glass left off and the crusty snow began.

There was a shout of approval and cheers and congratulatory smacks on the back, but the circle did not break and their expressions did not ease. They hunched over their hatred, cradling it jealously. It was a malignant, ugly thing to see. Kate felt sick, and it wasn't her wound. "Ladies, I think you'd better head on home. You're not driving yourselves, are you?"

Enid giggled, and hiccupped. "Hell, no, Bernie took all our keys away. We hitched a ride in."

"Have you got a ride home?" That stumped them. "Well," Kate said, "go on up to the post office. Ralph'll find somebody going your way."

Enid shrugged and grinned, pushing a hand of hair out of her eyes. "Okay."

As the circle began to break up, Kate couldn't resist

saying, "McAniff didn't kill Lisa Getty."

"What?"

"The cops tested McAniff's rifle. The bullet that killed Lisa Getty came from a different rifle."

She watched them carefully, but once they believed her, the response was collectively and, so far as Kate could see, completely surprised. Enid was the first to recover from the news, and she waved a dismissing hand. "Doesn't matter. Whoever did it, did the whole Park a favor."

That seemed to be the general consensus, and the women stumbled off, crashing through the trees with a fine disregard for either environmental preservation or personal safety.

Kate stood where she was, breathing deeply, trying to quell her roiling stomach. She had known Lisa was disliked among her own sex in the Park, but until today she had had no idea just how much. Her skin crawled and she wished she could take a bath. She raised her head, fixing her gaze on the small patch of sky the treetops allowed to show through.

A branch cracked behind her, and she whirled, her heart thumping.

Mutt's ruff expanded. Kate straightened and put a calming hand on her head.

Lottie was rooted in place, as if she had grown there among the scrub spruce and mountain hemlock and diamond willow, gathering her own rings of age over the short summers and the long winters. Her eyes were squeezed shut. Her pale skin looked waxen. She was as still and as hushed as the trees clustered thickly around her, abetting her silence.

That silence felt reverent but less than serene. "Lottie," Kate said, her voice a bare thread of sound. She cleared her throat, the sound rasping across the stillness. "I'm sorry you had to see that." She paused. "Lottie, you shouldn't be here."

The urgency in her voice got through. Lottie stirred. Her blue eyes opened, and she looked around. It took her a moment to focus, and when she did, her gaze fixed on the bandage on Kate's right temple, and then slid past without comment or question.

"Lottie," Kate said, "go home. Lisa's dead. You can't change that by hanging around here. It's not . . ." She hesitated, searching for the right word. "It's not healthy. I'll . . ." Again she hesitated. "I'll take care of this. Go on home now."

No response. Kate swore beneath her breath and looked around for inspiration. The surrounding trees presented a blank face in solidarity with Lottie. Kate decided to go for shock value. "I hear Lisa was seeing something of Max Chaney before she died."

The instantaneous change of expression on Lottie's usually stolid face astounded her. The skin reddened, the lips drew back into a snarl. Lottie's hands curled into claws, and Kate felt all the hair on the back of her neck rise. Mutt took a pace forward, getting between the two woman, facing Lottie and uttering one sharp, warning bark.

"Okay, Mutt," Kate said, putting a hand on the dog's back. "It's all right, girl. It's okay." She looked up at Lottie, and given their difference in height it was quite a way up, which Kate was aware of as never before. "Isn't it?" Lottie didn't reply, and Kate repeated, "Isn't it okay, Lottie?"

Still with that near-snarl on her face, Lottie looked from the dog to Kate and back again. Some of the tension went out of her. Her hands uncurled. "No, it's not okay, Kate," she said in her dull, thick voice. "It's not okay, and it's never going to be okay again."

She left, crashing blindly and indifferently through the trees, breaking branches off with her shoulders and crushing last year's seedlings beneath her boots. Kate, shaken down to her core for the second time in the

space of half an hour, retraced her path through trees that seemed a lot less hostile to her exit than they had to her entrance.

The seat of the Jag felt steady beneath her, and she leaned forward over the handlebars, her eyes closed, thinking hard. Max Chaney. Max Chaney, who had taken Mark Miller's place in the Parks Service when the latter had been killed the year before. Opening her eyes, she sat up straight and asked Mutt, "How about a trip up to the Step? We can stop at Neil's on the way."

In fact they made several stops on the way up to Park Service headquarters, at small homesteads scattered along the rough track that once was had been a roadbed, when the Kanuyaq & Northern Railroad ran between the copper and silver mines in the foothills of the Quilak Mountains and the port of Cordova on the coast of Prince William Sound. It was maintained only during the summer, and the half-frozen, broken surface of ice and mud was rutted and mushy. It was slow going, and sometimes Mutt had to walk while Kate got off and pushed their way out of yet another rut.

At the first homestead, a one-room cabin in the middle of a clearing still littered with the stumps of newly fallen trees, they were greeted with a sullen hostility that Kate wisely ignored. "Neil," she said patiently, "you know and I know what you've got growing out back. It's what's growing out back of half a dozen homesteads that I know of up and down this road. Because the troopers haven't spotted it from the air yet doesn't mean they couldn't, if someone gave them a tip as to where to look. Five'll get you ten Chopper Jim knows all about it already, and just hasn't had the time or the inclination to bother. If someone makes a complaint, he'll have to." She waited.

The white, ropey scar that bisected her throat was just visible in the opening of her collar. It began to itch

beneath his fixed gaze. "Lisa Getty was a competitor, Neil," Kate said, still patient. "Somebody killed her, and it wasn't McAniff." Jack may have wanted to keep Lisa's murder quiet, but he hadn't been shot at. Kate was done with discretion.

"You think I did it?" Neil, a burly, ponytailed man, said with a glower.

"You tell me. Where were you that morning?"

"I was here."

"Did you have company?"

He hesitated, and shook his head.

But Kate saw that hesitation and snapped, "Dammit, Neil, I don't care if you were making a sell. I'm not going to turn you or the buyer in if you were. Somebody killed Lisa Getty, and it wasn't Roger McAniff. Who was here that morning? Who's your alibi? I'll talk to them, and if I'm satisfied they're telling the truth, that'll be the end of it. Come on, Neil, you know my word's good."

He hesitated a moment longer and then said with patent reluctance, "Jeff Talbot came by that morning. He bought a couple lids and split."

"What time?"

He shrugged. "Ten. Maybe ten-thirty."

Which would not have left Neil enough time to make the scene of Lisa's murder and home again to sell dope to Jeff Talbot.

As she left the cabin, Kate eyed the gun rack above the door. It held a twelve-gauge, pump-action shotgun, much like her own, with enough firepower to take the heart out of most predators, especially the two-legged kind. The homesteader in her approved, if the investigator in her deplored this further evidence in support of Neil's innocence. She hadn't seen any other firearms inside. He could have tossed it down a convenient abandoned mine shaft, but she didn't think so. Neil Miles was representative of the Park's resident dope growers, a group collectively notorious for a nonviolent lifestyle.

The guy was a vegetarian, for God's sake. However greatly provoked, Kate couldn't see how someone who, when he couldn't bring himself to shoot a moose if he were starving to death, could shoot a human being in support of the law of supply and demand. No, she concluded gloomily, Neil might have given Lisa a carnation and a copy of the Bhagavad-Gita, but he wouldn't have shot her.

"What do you want to bet he reads Thoreau?" she asked Mutt.

Mutt yawned.

Neil Miles's homestead was perched on top of a rising swell of land in the middle of a long, wide valley swept smooth by glacial recession. The soil was dark and rich, and if the summers were short this far north, the summer days were eighteen hours long and, this far inland, hot. The moisture-laden winds off the Gulf of Alaska wrung themselves out against the southern slopes of the Quilaks, and the resulting summer rains were nourishing without being torrential. You could grow anything in the space of a Green Valley's short, hot summer, and the homesteaders did, and more than one grew it for resale. On that cheery thought Kate pressed the Jag's starter and half-rode, half-pushed her way out of Neil's front yard.

After her fourth stop and another interview identical to the previous three, Kate made straight for the Step. The higher they climbed, the colder it became and the smoother the track, and the last few miles went fast, switchbacks and all. They emerged onto a plateau, a flat, treeless step of land three thousand feet up from the valley and anywhere from six to sixteen thousand feet below the jagged peaks at its back. The Step was a mile in length and three thousand feet across and had an airstrip running down its exact center. An old Cessna Kate recognized as the one George Perry had been working on two days before was lifting off one

end of the strip as she emerged onto the plateau. She waved, and the plane rocked a hello before dropping its right wing in an abrupt bank toward the mountains.

South of the Step lay the Kanuyaq River and civilization, or what passed for it in the Park. North of the Step lay the Quilak Mountain Range. At one end of the airstrip, Park headquarters was a clump of prefabricated buildings that housed representatives of every government bureaucracy that had anything to do with federal land management and natural resources, as well as a few that had nothing to do with either. Coexisting in frequently unfriendly proximity were the U.S. Department of Wildlife, the Alaska State Department of Fish and Game, the Alaska State Division of Mines, the Alaska State Division of Forestry, the National Oceanic and Atmospheric Administration, the Bureau of Land Management, and last, but as Dan O'Brian would certainly tell you most emphatically, not least, the National Park Service.

Presiding over this cacophonous, controlled brawl was Dan O'Brian. As head ranger he was in nominal charge of keeping the sports fishermen from assaulting the subsistence fishermen, both groups from attacking the commercial fishermen, and all three of them from rising up in concert to do away with the grossly outnumbered but resolute agents of the Department of Fish and Game. It was enough to induce paranoia in the most well-balanced and even-tempered individual, which was probably why when Kate tracked Dan down, she found him howling obscenities behind the closed door of his otherwise empty office.

"Taken up primal scream therapy, Danny boy?"

Dan O'Brian never did anything halfway. When he hated, he hated, and when he loved, he loved, and he adored Kate. His voice broke in mid-howl. Jumping to his feet, he came around the desk and swept her up into a rough embrace and a smacking kiss.

"Watch yourself, bozo," she said, fending him off, "or I'll sic Mutt on you."

He leaned over, grabbed Mutt's head between two rough-skinned hands and gave her a smacking kiss, too. Mutt's eyes closed halfway and she almost purred. "That dog's heels are even rounder than yours," Dan observed. "What're you two doing up here this early?" His gaze sharpened. "You looking for work? We got half a dozen fire watch positions opening up in another month."

Kate raised an eyebrow. "You expecting a lot of fires this season? It's only April, Dan."

"It's been a bad winter, and I hear salmon prices are going to drop even further this year than last." He made a face and spread his hands. "You know how it is. Times are tough. When times get tough people get broke. Before long somebody heads out into the Park and finds themselves a stand of spruce infested with spruce beetles and strikes a match, and shortly thereafter goes to work smoke jumping for the Department of Interior." He gave a fatalistic shrug. "It feeds the kids."

Kate eyed him with something approaching respect. "You're sitting pretty calm at the prospect of thousands of Park acres going up in flames."

"Not calm. Reconciled to my fate, maybe. Anyway, you want a job?"

Kate felt the weight of the envelope lying against her breast and smiled to herself. "Not this year."

"Damn. We could use someone on the line that knows a smoke trail from morning fog." He sighed.

"No, I'm up here for something else entirely."

Something in her voice alerted him. He returned to his seat, folded his hands on his desk and regarded her, at attention. "What's going on?"

"You heard about McAniff's little shooting spree down in Niniltna, I assume."

His face darkened. "Who hasn't?" He shook his head. "Bunch of good people dead, for no earthly reason that

anyone can discover. Crazy bastard." He eyed her curiously. "Chopper Jim said McAniff made a try at you and you nailed him."

"Sort of."

"Good girl."

"Thanks. Mutt deserves most of the credit."

"Good *girl*," Dan told Mutt, unknowingly echoing Kate's very words that day. Mutt's tail thumped the floor enthusiastically. "What's the going rate for apprehending homicidal maniacs these days?"

"The grateful thanks of John Q. Public."

"Lucky you. So what's the problem? You caught McAniff, murder weapon in hand. From what I hear, he hasn't denied doing any of it."

"On the contrary."

"Bragging about it, is he?" Dan said distastefully.

"Nonstop, from what I hear."

"Sick."

"Yeah."

"So what *is* the problem?" He gave her a shrewd look. "There is one, isn't there?"

"The problem is, one of the victims was killed by a bullet from a different rifle."

Sound seemed to seep out of the room, leaving an empty, hollow feeling behind.

"Jesus H. Christ on a crutch," Dan said at last, slowly, the syllables dropping into the silence like rocks down a deep well. "We got *another* mad killer on the loose with a 30.06?"

"So it seems."

He seemed to see the bandage on her temple for the first time, and his eyes narrowed. He raised an eyebrow, and she nodded. "I think so." She raised a hand to forestall his next question. "No, I didn't see them."

"Where were you?"

"Lisa Getty was the one shot with a different rifle. I was tossing her boat down on the river. They got me on deck."

He sat upright. "Lisa Getty?" She nodded, and he said with utter loathing, "Whoever killed that bitch did everything in the Park on four legs a favor."

Kate sighed. "Great. Another prospective charter member for the Grateful Lisa Getty's Dead Fan Club. What, specifically, did you have against her?"

"Nothing I could prove or I'd'a jailed that bitch long since." Dan was a tall man with bushy, carrot-colored hair, blue eyes that usually twinkled with good humor and an open, freckled face that was usually smiling. There was no smile and no twinkle now. "I followed her up into the Quilaks twice and found at least half a dozen dead black bear both goddam times."

"Ah. Bladders gone?"

"Yep, and the fur and the meat just left there, wasted."

"Not wasted, exactly," Kate murmured, "coyotes and foxes got to eat, too."

Dan carried on, unheeding. "God, how I hate that! I could live with the poaching, game has to be regularly harvested to keep the population down so it doesn't run out of feed, but it's the waste that pisses me off. And this time of year is the worst. Jesus, the goddam bears've been sleeping all winter, their coats are the best they'll ever be, they've just woke up and they haven't had a chance to get at the fish yet so their meat tastes the best it ever will, and that bitch shoots 'em and guts 'em for the fucking *bladders* and leaves the rest there to rot! Can you believe it?"

The question was obviously rhetorical. Kate, having been acquainted with the residents of the Park for a lot longer than Dan, who as a ten-year veteran was a comparative newcomer, wisely refrained from answering.

"And I *know*," he added, "I *know* she had a hand in that sudden drop in sea otter population we had in the Ikamag Fjords last year. Plus I'm positive she's been flying into the Ahlbach seal rookery. Bitch was

a goddam one-woman meat grinder."

"I hear black bear bladders are fetching a good price."

His spleen temporarily vented, Dan gave a gloomy nod. "Anywhere from six hundred to a thousand bucks apiece on the Asian black market. And why not? Any Hong Kong chemist'll tell you, ground bladder of black bear'll cure anything from impotence to influenza."

Kate raised her eyebrows. "Nice work if you can get it."

"Like hell." Dan glared at her suspiciously. "And don't let it give you any ideas, either, Kate. We got a stable population of bear in this friggin' Park and I'd like to keep it that way."

Kate widened her eyes at Dan, the picture of innocence. He snorted, and she smothered a smile. "You sure Lisa was the one doing the poaching?"

"I'm sure. Like I said, I had my suspicions and I followed her a couple times. She left bear carcasses on her trail the way moose leave nuggets. I was dying to bust her; I just hadn't been able to catch her in the act."

"Odd," Kate said in a ruminative voice.

"What is?"

"Oh, I heard one of your rangers was spending some time with her." She met his eyes. "That his idea, or yours?"

Beneath her fascinated gaze Dan swelled up to twice his normal size and exploded in a burst of rage. "One of *my* rangers was fucking that bitch? Which one? Tell me! I'll kill him! Which one? Goddammit, Kate, if you know, you'd better say!"

Just for meanness Kate said, "It was Max Chaney," and Dan erupted out of his chair and stamped over to the door and shouted Chaney's name down the hall. When there was no reply, the door slammed shut with a force that reverberated up through the legs of Kate's chair. Mutt came to her feet, alarmed.

Simmering, Dan sat down again, very erect. A long, timid silence ensued, broken by the cautious creak of the opening door. An eye peered through the crack. "You bellowed, boss?"

"Where's that fucker Chaney?"

"Not on the premises, boss," the voice said, gaining confidence now that its owner knew he wasn't the one on the carpet.

"Well find him or find out where the hell he is!"

The door shut promptly, and feet beat rapidly down the hall and out of earshot.

"I remember once," Kate said, "when I was working for the D.A.'s office, they made me take this class called Interaction Management. It was all about how to supervise one's employees, to teach them how to get along with their fellow workers and encourage them to realize their full potential." She looked at Dan. "Wonder why they didn't call you in as a guest lecturer."

The door crashed back against the wall, and a tall young man, thin almost to the point of emaciation stood breathing heavily in the doorway, his exhalations causing his magnificent handlebar mustache to ruffle like seaweed in a strong current. "You better come, boss."

Dan was on his feet, his eyes fixed on the other man. "What's the matter, Kevin?"

Kevin's face was paper white, and he was shaking so hard Kate thought she could hear his bones rattling together beneath their negligible layer of skin. "It's Chaney, boss. I think he's dead."

Max Chaney was dead all right, as dead as a bullet through the forehead can make one. It was a small, dark, perfectly round hole, with very little blood. He lay on his back in front of an open window in his tiny bedroom, as if the shot had caught him as he leaned out to take a breath of spring air. If so, it had been his last.

"Stop," Kate said sharply from the doorway. "Don't touch anything else. Everybody out. You, too, Dan. Kevin? Get on the radio and put in a call to Chopper Jim. Tell him there's a man down, dead, same M.O. as Lisa Getty, looks like the same weapon. Tell him to get on the horn to Anchorage and get a forensics team up here *crash*. Got that?" Kate had to repeat herself. "Have you got that, Kevin?"

"Man dead, same M.O. as Lisa Getty, forensics team crash," Kevin repeated numbly.

"After you talk to Jim, try to raise Bobby Clark on the radio. He might not be there but Jack Morgan probably will be." Kevin hung fire where he was, staring at Chaney's body with dilated eyes and a slowly greening complexion. Kate put a hand on his shoulder and gave him a little nudge. He seemed to come awake, and turned to stumble through the crowd gathered around the door.

Nothing in life makes a body look as awkward as death, not even sex. Chaney's limbs looked broken where they lay, as if death had somehow rearranged them to grow out at odd angles. His brown hair was neatly parted and combed, his skin was whiter than Kevin's, and his eyes, wide, thickly lashed and brown in color, stared at the ceiling with a puzzled look. Waving back Dan, whose shock had given way to a cold, tight-lipped fury, Kate knelt next to the remains of Max Chaney and with gentle fingers closed his eyes. They were lukewarm to the touch, and somehow less firm than living flesh. He hadn't been dead long; his arm moved easily when she flexed the elbow.

She controlled an inner shudder and rose. "Can you lock this door, Dan?"

Outside the building Mutt met her with a worried frown. Kate patted her head absently, which made the dog look even more worried. Dan, standing next to them and swearing steadily, broke off long enough to demand, "Well? What do we do now?"

Kate, staring at the peaked heads of the Quilak Mountains, didn't answer. He nudged her and repeated the question.

Starting, she stared at him for a moment, as if recalled only by force from a place far away. "Wait for the trooper. Jack Morgan'll be along, too; he flew in this morning. Tell them everything you know."

"That won't take long," he growled.

"From the looks of things I'd guess the shot came from that stand of hemlocks just up the strip. Don't go over there, and don't let anybody else go over there. Let Jim and his team get to it first before you track up the snow."

"They're not going to find anything; it's been melting faster than butter on a hot plate the last week. Wait a minute," he added as she started toward her snow machine, "where do you think you're going?"

"I've got to talk to someone. I'm sorry, Danny boy, but it's important." She mounted the machine and started the engine.

"Goddammit, Shugak, I'd like to know what's more important than answering a lot of dumb questions from that dumbass trooper from Tok!"

"The only reason you don't like Chopper Jim is because he beat you to my cousin Martha," she yelled over the noise of the engine. "Come on, Mutt!"

Mutt, with an apologetic look over her shoulder at Dan, hopped up behind Kate, and the machine lurched off down the mountain.

"Women!" Dan O'Brian said, with a loathing that encompassed mistress and dog, and set about the task of calming down twenty-five slightly hysterical Park workers, most of whom had never heard a shot fired in anger before in their lives, unless they were Fish and Game agents.

eight

BY running the engine flat out Kate made it Step to town in less than an hour. She was lucky and met Bernie at the door of the Niniltna High School gymnasium. "Bernie, hold up! I want to talk to you."

"Can't stop now, I got a potlatch to go to."

"I didn't know you came to potlatches," Kate said, momentarily diverted.

"I didn't come, I was commanded," he said. "Didn't you hear? Ekaterina put the word out—the whole Park is supposed to be here. Besides, the first game of the tournament begins right after."

"What tournament?" she asked innocently.

"Ha, ha. What happened?" he asked, nodding at her bandage. "Jack clip you one?"

"Ha, ha," she replied. "Bernie, I need to—"

He waved her through the door and the words died on her lips.

The gym was large and rectangular, with a high ceiling, a hardwood floor and bleachers on one side. From one backboard hung an American flag, from the other the maple leaf of Canada. Centered on the opposite wall was a sign that read in large, black, plain-spoken letters, "Please Honor And Respect That This Is An Alcohol Free Event." Beneath the sign half a dozen long tables placed end to end were stacked with platters and casseroles and bowls and trays, each featuring the owner's very own

135

special recipe for fish head stew or caribou sausage or blood stew or boiled moose tongue or muktuk or kulich or pashka. Drums were beating as Kate entered, the crowd in the bleachers spilled out around the walls of the room, and Ekaterina Moonin Shugak was calling down the tribes, and everything else was driven out of Kate's head.

"Inupiat!" The drum beat on, the response was tepid, and Ekaterina said, her deep voice amplified by the microphone, "Inupiat! Come on, get out here! You know if you don't I'll come up there and get you out!"

Half a dozen people groaned and laughed and climbed down out of the bleachers to join the costumed tribal dancers on the floor. They crouched over bent knees, stepping from one foot to the other and shaking their hands in time to the beat.

"Athabascan!"

An old, old man in beaded buckskins and wearing hearing aids in both ears made his slow and stately way out onto the floor. He was using a walker, but he had his dancing slippers on, made of buckskin and heavily beaded.

Bernie noticed Kate standing very still. "What is it?"

She took a breath. "It's Chief William. From Tanana. He almost never leaves his house nowadays. Emaa must have asked him to come as a personal favor to her."

"Who's Chief William?"

"He's the oldest chief of any tribe in Alaska. He's probably the oldest Alaskan there is, for that matter."

"How old is he?"

"He was born in 1867. The year Russia sold Alaska to the United States."

Bernie whistled, a long, low whistle. "That'd make him—what? A hundred and . . . ?"

"A hundred and twenty-five."

"And still dancing," Bernie said, marveling. "I should be in such good shape when I'm a hundred and twenty-five."

Kate shook herself, resisting her awe. "He was born somewhere up around Ahtna, way before there was a town. He doesn't have a birth certificate, so they can only guess at his age. He's probably younger."

"He could be older," Bernie suggested.

Kate's breath expelled on a short laugh. "So he could. I never thought of that."

The other dancers made way for the old chief's slow but steady progress out into the middle of the floor. As small and wrinkled as he was, as hampered by the walker as he was, his dancing was deliberate, dignified and kept to the beat of the drums, which had slowed to accommodate him. His voice was small and weak when he called out, but somehow the words echoed clearly across the big room and brought responding shouts from everywhere in the crowd. Accompanying him was a young boy of ten or twelve, wearing jeans and Nike tennis shoes and clutching an eagle feather in each fist. He was a little clumsy but enthusiastic as he followed his great-great-grandfather around the floor, stamping his feet and shaking his eagle feathers.

"I didn't know there were so many of you," Bernie said, staring in wonder at the crowded floor.

"Not so many," Kate said, too low for him to hear. "So few." As always, the dance of her ancestors stirred opposing emotions in her. There was much joy in the sight of so many of her people together in one place, celebrating their heritage. There was as much sorrow. They were so few, barely enough to fill this gym.

Bernie looked from the dancers to the short, lithe woman standing next to him, her pensive expression emphasizing the beauty of her flat, high cheekbones, the clear, light brown, almond-shaped eyes with the hint of the epicanthic fold in the crease of the upper lid, the wide mouth, held firmly, even a bit primly, the clear, golden skin stretched tautly over good bones, the shining black fall of hair braided severely back from her face. She

looked like a walking, breathing advertisement for "How the West Was Won," except that if Kate had been there he wasn't sure it would have been. He ran through what he knew about Kate Shugak. She never touched alcohol. She could turn her hand to any task in the Park and perform it in an efficient and competent manner. Her sense of humor was strong. He had seen the sense of responsibility she felt toward the people of the Park, which warred with her veneration for personal freedom, the ability to think and do as one chose. He had also seen the way people of the Park looked at Kate, with respect verging on awe. Their voices dropped when they spoke of her; they drew back where she walked. Her deeds were legend, from her apprehension of the child molester that had resulted in the scar across her neck, to the brutal if efficient ejection of the bootlegger last winter. Abel Int-Hout's suicide four months ago and the two murders that had preceded it were still being talked about over the bar at the Roadhouse, and with each retelling Kate's part in the events became ever larger than life.

Now, Bernie looked at her and for the first time saw a Native Alaskan, a hard, tough descendant of a thousand years of Great Land Darwinism. "What's he wearing?" he said, in a voice soft enough not to break the spell. "Chief William. It looks like something out of a museum."

"It probably should be in one. It's a hunter's tunic and leggings."

"Made out of what?"

"Tanned caribou hide, probably. Maybe moose."

"What're the decorations?"

"Beads and dentalium shells."

"The earrings?"

"More beads and dentalium shells. The nosepin's a dentalium shell, too."

Chief William paused, one hand on his walker. With the other he pulled out what looked like a long, brown, hollow tube. "What's that?" Bernie said.

"A sucking tube. Made of antler. Shamans use them to suck the evil spirits from the sick."

The tube raised to his lips, Chief William sucked in, once, twice, three times. The drums picked up speed, and the crowd shouted their approval. Chief William put the tube away and made his stately way back to his seat.

"Aleut!" Ekaterina called.

A shriek went up fit to raise the roof and half the bleachers took to the floor in a stamping, shaking mass.

"Koniag!"

A woman moved out from the crowd to dance directly in front of Ekaterina. She wore a skullcap made from strings of brightly-colored glass beads that hung in fringes over her eyes and down her back, and an ivory-and-feather finger mask on each hand. The beads swung and sparkled in the light, the feathers on the finger masks swept wide arcs through the air. Her face was broad and bronzed, her eyes merry, her hair long and straight with reddish gleams beneath the light. Her movements were deft and graceful and she looked delightful, and if her flirtatious, up-from-under glances at the male dancers were any indication, she knew it.

"Hawaiian!" Ekaterina called. "Come on, Keoki!"

An enormous man wearing a high, plumed helmet and a floor-length cloak made of brilliant yellow and red feathers took to the floor and hurled himself into a hula, and there was a roar of approval.

"The black man!"

The circle of dancers drew back and looked around. No one came forward. The drummer whacked the drum louder, and Ekaterina repeated in a voice pitched to be heard in Oregon, "The black man!"

Bobby wheeled out of the crowd amid a roar of approval. "See, Bobby, I knew you were here!" Ekaterina called.

Bobby moved the wheels of his chair backward and forward with the beat of the drums and walked his head

and shoulders like an Egyptian. A circle of high-stepping, gyrating dancers formed around his chair, and he threw back his head and howled, his black face gleaming with sweat, his mouth split wide in a grin.

"The white man!" There was a whoop and a holler and one lone Rebel yell and a dozen more people took to the floor.

"I thought a potlatch was for naming a baby," Bernie said to Kate, raising his voice over the increasing roar of the crowd.

"It is. It's for a lot of things."

"It's like a, what, religious rite?"

Kate shook her head. "It's more social than religious. In the old days, it was so the people could come together and help share the work and the food. A village would throw a potlatch to celebrate the raising of a new totem pole, or a big chief would have one to show how rich and powerful he was, or maybe a couple's parents would throw one for their wedding." She smiled. "I remember when I was a little girl, my cousin Martin's parents had a potlatch to name him when he was a year old, and another when he turned five and had his first haircut, and a third for when he shot his first caribou." She sighed. "Then, when my Aunt Mary and my Uncle Bob were cheated out of their homestead by a bank in Fairbanks, their children had a potlatch to show them how many people loved them, to take the hurt away. You can have a potlatch for anything, when it comes from deep down in your heart."

"And this one?"

"This one's for the ten people who were killed here last month."

"I thought they were all white."

Kate gave him an impatient look. "It wouldn't matter one way or another if they were. They lived here. They were our neighbors."

"Even Mac Devlin?" Bernie asked with the lift of an eyebrow.

"Even Mac Devlin," Kate said firmly. "Nobody likes him and I wouldn't be surprised if somebody shot at him again someday, but he was part of the event, the . . . the tragedy, if you will. And, not that it matters, but Tina Weiss was a quarter Aleut. I think we were related in a shirttail sort of way through my father's family in Cordova. And the Jorgensens had lived here forever, and Pat's brothers still do. And who wouldn't grieve over the deaths of two newlyweds and their unborn baby?" Kate was speaking dispassionately now. "Emaa had this potlatch to call their spirits back one more time, to remember them with joy instead of sorrow, to celebrate their life and friendship, and then let them go."

Potlatches, she could have added, were also held to put the guests under obligation to the host. She looked across the room at Ekaterina, broad, ageless face creased in a wide grin, and thought, No, Emaa never does anything for only one reason.

The drums gathered force, and as each individual dancer took to the floor and fell in with the rhythm, the crowd began to take on the look of a single, joyous entity. Bobby's Fifth Annual Celebration of the Twentieth Anniversary of the Tet Offensive had been a dirge lamenting useless death and a senseless war. By contrast, the potlatch was a paean to life and to those who lived it, a remembrance of the dead, an act of homage. If the dancers mourned the passing of the dead, they also rejoiced in the lives those individuals had lived, and rejoiced as well, unashamed, in their own. Kate thought of the quilters and the mushers and the parishioners and the belly dancers at the Roadhouse on Wednesday, and smiled suddenly. Even The Rite of the Middle Finger, that Flipping Off of Fate by Big Bumpers who had made it all the way to the top and lived whole and entire to tell the tale, was part and parcel of the same service.

Ekaterina threw back her head and called in a voice that rang off the rafters, "Everybody!"

"This is incredible, Kate," Bernie said. "I've never seen anything like this." There was no reply and he looked around. "Kate?"

She was down on the floor, moving among the dancers with fluid grace. Her legs were bent at the knee, her arms were up, and she leaned forward, stepping from one foot to the other, always in time with the beat of the drums. The drums became louder, until they filled the room up to the ceiling and bounced back down again. Kate threw back her head and called, to whom or to what Bernie didn't know. Half a dozen people called back, and the beat increased in speed and decibel level. Chief William's great-great-grandson tossed Kate an eagle feather, and she caught it deftly in her right hand and used it to draw graceful pictures in the air as she danced. The Koniag girl threw her a finger mask, and she slipped the carved ivory-and-feather hoop over her left index finger. Her braid loosened, and her hair fell free and hid the white bandage on her temple, and she began to toss her head and throw her long black hair back and forth. She lunged at a group of dancers, calling to them, and they lunged and called back. The boy with the eagle feather and the Nikes caught up with her, and for a while they danced together, Kate slowing down so that he could keep up. She turned and danced away; he followed. Another fell into line, a third, and soon all the dancers were stamping their feet and shaking their hands in a line that snaked around the floor and doubled back on itself half a dozen times. Kate led the way, up the floor and down, in and out of the corners, around the tables and back again.

On the floor, Kate's pulse seemed to beat in time with the beat of the drums, her breath to come and go with them, her steps dictated by them. The drums guided her through the dance with a firm hand, taking over her body and leaving her mind free to grieve.

Abel. She had not thought of him, or had tried not to, in months. Abel, her uncle-by-choice, her uncle-by-honor, who had died if not by her hand, then as a result of actions she had put in motion. He had guided her steps throughout her childhood as the drums guided her steps now, had taught her everything she knew of woodcraft, of hunting and fishing. His missing presence was a constant ache at the back of her mind. Suddenly she saw him, standing at the edge of the crowd, his grizzled old face grinning at her, his faded blue eyes twinkling, as if to say, "Well, girl? Ready to do a little poaching with the old man?" He turned as if to go, and she faltered slightly, and then the beat of the drums caught her up and swept her away.

She saw Pat and Becky Jorgensen, hand in hand, smiling warmly at her, their fingers smeared with ink and marked with paper cuts from sorting their neighbors' mail. The thin, intense figure of Steven Syms stared over at her with a fanatical expression. He'd been a born-again Baptist type, Kate remembered, who never went anywhere without a Bible and who had staged a one-man protest demonstration, with sign, in front of the Roadhouse when a movement to reform Alaska's twenty-year-old legal abortion law was quashed in the state legislature. Next to him, Lisa Getty, blond and blue-eyed, slender and seductive, smiled the smile that enticed and mocked at the same time. Max Chaney, appropriately enough, stood on her other side, looking around with a puzzled expression, so new to the company that he did not yet understand his presence in it. Other figures appeared dimly, figures she knew must be the Longstaffs and the Weisses, coming to bid her farewell.

She strained to see her mother, her father, but it had been too long since their deaths, and nothing was left of their spirits on earth except what she carried within her.

The drums began to slow and ease in volume, and Kate's movements slowed and eased with them. The song ended on a long fade, Kate's dance with a last, graceful

flight of eagle feather through the air. The music stopped as she came to a halt before Chief William. She reached for his gnarled, twisted old hand and, bending forward from the waist, held it for a moment to her forehead. She returned the finger mask to the Koniag dancer and held both hands out, palms up and eagle feather lying across them, to the boy. She said something to him, and he blushed and ducked his head.

Bernie was awed, by the dance, by the spirit it invoked, even in him, a practicing cynic, the only philosophy a working bartender could hold to and survive. "That was the most beautiful thing I've ever seen in my life," he told Kate when she returned to his side.

Her face was flushed and she was out of breath. She laughed at him, and then he saw her smile fade and a guarded wariness replace the joy in her eyes. He turned and saw the square, stately figure of Ekaterina Moonin Shugak approaching, and in that moment he remembered something else about Kate Shugak. She didn't get along with her grandmother.

"Emaa," Kate said, inclining her head stiffly. Her temple gave a vicious throb.

"Katya," her grandmother said. She gave a regal, dismissing nod in Bernie's general direction. Bernie, amused, had watched the stout old woman make her progress through the crowd, smiling at someone, stopping to shake hands with someone else, holding up a baby and exclaiming over its beauty, in a manner that reminded him irresistibly of Elizabeth II of England outside Buckingham Palace. He managed now to remove himself from her presence without quite bowing and backing away.

"Bernie, wait," Kate said, "I need to talk to you. It's why I came. Can we go—"

He raised a dismissive hand. "Later."

"Not later, now. Bernie, it's important. I have to talk to—"

"Whatever it is'll keep. I've got a team to psych up."

"I am glad to see you here, dancing with your people," the old woman said to Kate.

Kate watched Bernie's back moving rapidly in the opposite direction and swore under her breath. She almost went after him but couldn't quite bring herself to turn her back on her grandmother and walk away, and cursed again. "I enjoyed it, emaa," she said out loud. Determined to give the devil her due, she added, "This potlatch was a good idea."

"It was the right thing to do," her namesake said simply.

"Yes," Kate agreed. "And a good thing, for all of us. Friends," she added, emphasizing the word, "as well as family."

There fell an awkward silence. At least for Kate it was awkward. The last time Ekaterina Moonin Shugak might have felt awkward was during the birth of her thirteenth child, some thirty years previous. Kate doubted it. Ekaterina Moonin Shugak ruled her family, the Niniltna Tribal Association, the Park, the Alaska Federation of Natives and much of the Alaska state legislature with the same firm, unshakable, unfumbling hand with which she would have ruled Kate, had Kate let her, and she was never, ever awkward.

Kate cleared her throat. "Well, I came to see someone, emaa. I'd better get to it."

The old woman delayed her, touching a forefinger to the bandage at her granddaughter's temple. "You've been hurt."

Kate shrugged away. "It is nothing."

Ekaterina's hand dropped back to her side. "Have you heard from Axenia?"

Kate went on alert. "Yes."

"How is she?"

"She's fine, emaa. Jack found her an apartment and a roommate. She's enjoying her job. And she's enrolled

in an accounting class at the University of Alaska. She sounded very happy the last time I talked to her."

Kate couldn't help the defensive sound her words took on at the last. The old woman did not reply, but her silence was immensely eloquent, at least to Kate. "Well, if that's all, I'd better get going."

"Katya."

"What!"

Her grandmother looked mildly surprised at her tone, and Kate was immediately ashamed of herself and as immediately determined not to show it. "I only wanted to say, Katya, that you may have been right about Axenia."

Kate's jaw dropped slightly, and the old woman pressed her advantage. "She was unhappy here. If she is happy in the city, perhaps it was good for her to move there. If she had stayed home, who knows? Your mother . . ." Ekaterina didn't finish her sentence.

Kate regarded her with a slowly lightening expression, and unfortunately Ekaterina chose that moment to add, "Besides, the tribe does not need weaklings. There are few enough of us left. Those that remain must be strong."

Kate stiffened. "Axenia demonstrated her strength when she had the courage to recognize she didn't want to live here. She demonstrated her determination when she fought your disapproval to move to Anchorage, and she demonstrated her courage when she moved away from everything and everyone she knew, to a place with no friends or family."

"She abandoned her culture," Ekaterina snapped back, and those watching from a discreet distance were struck by the similarity of their faces, one old, one young, both stubborn.

"Maybe not," Kate said, bristling. "Maybe she took her culture with her, to pass it on to those who weren't lucky enough to be raised in it."

"No real Aleut—"

"Define Aleut for me, emaa," Kate said in a voice that was almost a shout. "Are we talking about the Kanuyaq River Aleuts, most of whom are descended from Ninety-Niners as much as they are Alaskan Indians? Are we talking about the Kodiak Island Aleuts, who are descended from Russian *promishlyniki* as much as they are the Alutiiq? Or are we talking about our own family, which in only the last four generations includes a Russian cossack, a Jewish cobbler, a Norwegian fisherman, a Rhode Island whaler and a Cherokee chief? Axenia is as much one of us as you or I, emaa. Just because she chooses not to live in the Park doesn't make her any less an Aleut. Or any more a weakling."

She spun around on one heel and marched off, shoving her way through the crowd, now engaged in wrapping up the remaining food, breaking down the tables and clearing the floor for basketball action. She was angry and wasn't paying attention to where she was going.

"Whoa!" a male voice said when she ran full tilt into someone. Two hands caught at her arms to steady her.

She looked up, shoving the hair out of her eyes. "Oh. Hi, George. Sorry, I wasn't watching where I was going."

"No problem." He released her.

"You get your Koreans off okay?"

"Yeah, Lottie took them up." He grinned. "She didn't look any too happy about it, but I made her an offer she couldn't refuse."

Kate halted and stared at him. "Today?"

He nodded. "Just a couple hours ago."

"You stop to get permits?"

He looked surprised. "Of course. Dan issued them himself. We stopped on the Step long enough to check in with Park Service and then I kicked them out at the base camp."

"How's the weather?" she asked automatically, not really listening to his reply.

He shrugged. "Looking good for now, but who knows? We're talking Big Bump here. That mother changes moods the way Princess Di does clothes."

Someone called his name and he turned to answer. "Damn," Kate whispered. Then all her suspicions were true, and there was nothing she could do now to stop it all coming out. Someone bumped into her, jostling her out of her preoccupation. "Damn," she said, more loudly, "damn, damn, *damn,*" and shoved her way through the crowd toward the stairwell.

There was a long hall at the bottom of the stairs. She walked all the way down to the end, stopped in front of the door of the boys' locker room and banged on it with a clenched fist, venting her anger on the blank and innocent steel. The door opened and Stevie Kvasnikof's suspicious face appeared. "No girls allowed," he growled and would have slammed the door shut if she hadn't smacked her open palm against it and stiffened her arm.

"I want to talk to Eknaty."

"Eknaty who?" he said, thrusting his jaw forward. "There's no Eknaty in here."

"Eknaty Kvasnikof your brother, you idiot," she told him. "I know he's in there, he's the shining hope of Niniltna's second Class C state championship. Tell him I want to talk to him."

He glowered at her for a moment and then turned to yell. "Coach! Hey, Coach! Kate Shugak's out here!"

There was a chorus of young and rude male noises. Bernie shoved past Stevie and closed the door behind him. He stood in front of her with his hands on his hips. Any lingering, mellowing effects of the dancing upstairs had dissolved in the cold, bracing anticipation of competitive testosterone. "What do you want?" he demanded. "We got a game to play. If you want to talk to me, see me after."

"I don't want to talk to you, I want to talk to Eknaty," Kate said, patiently for her.

"Same thing. You want to talk to Eknaty, you see me after." He half turned and paused. "Why do you want to see him, anyway?"

"Max Chaney's been shot."

He froze. "What?"

"Max Chaney has been shot. He's dead."

He paled. "Like Lisa?"

She raised her eyebrows. "You know about Lisa?"

His eyes fell. "Enid told me." He looked up. "Was he? Was Max Chaney shot like Lisa?"

"It looks like it."

"Jesus." Bernie's eyes closed and he shook his head.

"I know," she said. "We can't go around anymore with our heads in the sand, hoping something will happen to make this all go away. The killer has killed twice now, has even had a try at me." She touched the bandage at her temple. His eyes widened. "You said Eknaty was pretty upset at Lisa's death. If he was odd-jobbing it for Lottie, he may have been there the morning Lisa got shot. He may have seen something. If I can find the rifle that shot her . . ." Her voice trailed away.

Their eyes met in perfect, if almost shamed, understanding. "All right," he said finally. "You can see him. After the game," he said, raising his hand to stop her when she reached for the door. "And for ten minutes only. I'm not having you play mind-fuck games with my star guard in the middle of the goddam state championship. And Kate," he said, raising one finger and poking it toward her with vicious emphasis, "if that kid's free-throw percentage falls after tonight, I'll be on you like stink on shit."

When Kate reentered the gym, the tables and food and signs had disappeared, the floor had been swept clean, and the dancers had abandoned the floor for the bleachers,

and were packed in together as tight as a salmon stream in July. The potlatch had left everyone feeling good, and the prospect of three solid days of basketball put the cap on everyone's enjoyment.

Of the half dozen teams from around the state, first up in the tournament's rotation were the Kanuyaq Kings against the Seldovia Sea Otters. Cheerleaders in letter sweaters and short skirts stamped and clapped and yelled and worked the crowd into a feeding frenzy. The Kings took to the floor in blue and gold, the Otters in red and white. The Kings' center was half a foot taller but the Otters' center wanted it more and Seldovia got the tip-off.

"Two points, big team, two points," the Otters' cheerleaders chanted. "Defense, defense!" the home crowd yelled. The Otters tried too hard and the guards took the ball down the court without waiting for the rest of their team to take position. The lay-up rolled around the rim and out of the basket and was recovered by a King forward who broke and ran with it. His slam went dunk and the crowd went wild. Galvanized, the Otters brought the ball back in and down the court, set up a tight man-to-man offense, worked the ball around the key until their center was clear and fed it to him the way momma feeds strained pears to baby, no nonsense and down the hatch. He pivoted and hooked it in, swish. "Oh, nice one!" Kate called involuntarily, and the crowd, appreciative of good basketball whoever was doing the playing, gave the Otters an enthusiastic hand.

No player on either team was very tall but all the players were quick, agile, and had a bad case of the wants to win. During the next half hour the lead changed hands with the ball. There was very little fouling and Eknaty Kvasnikof's legendary free throw ability was sidelined. Kate approved; she didn't want the Kings to give the ball away but if she wanted to see a fistfight she'd go to a hockey game. The score at the half was

40–41, and both teams looked it. The players hit the locker rooms and the crowd surged outside, to enjoy the cool night air and smoke and talk and recap each play of the first half with all the gravity of Jim McKay recapping an Olympic playoff. A group of young men was passing a pint bottle around, until one of them saw Kate. The bottle disappeared. She held them motionless with a fixed, bleak stare, until they decided they had business elsewhere.

In response to a short, sharp whistle, Mutt cantered around a corner, ears up and an expectant expression on her face. Kate fed her a handful of caribou steaks she'd pocketed from the buffet. "Sorry it's taking so long, girl."

Mutt, her mouth full of caribou, uttered a muffled 'woof' that gave Kate to understand that she was well on her way to being forgiven.

"Hey there, you dancing fool," somebody said, and she turned to find Bobby skidding dangerously across a thick layer of slush that was rapidly refreezing with each dropping degree of temperature. He half rolled, half slid to a stop next to her, barely missing her toes. Mutt sent a cold, yellow stare his way, and he said hastily, "Now you know I wouldn't dare to roll my chair across *your* toes, Mutt old girl. It has never been my ambition in life to serve as first course at a wolf banquet." He looked up at Kate, and she squatted down next to him, leaning against the arm of his chair. "You really know how to shake your booty, woman. You have unsuspected talents." She smiled with an effort, and he examined that smile. "You okay?"

On a long sigh, she said, "Max Chaney's been shot."

He nodded. "It's all over the crowd."

"Who told?" she said, annoyed.

He shrugged. "You know the bush telegraph. It was all over the Park a hour after. What are you going to do, Kate?"

"What I have to," she said, staring past him, unseeing. "What I should have done in the first place."

A big, large-knuckled hand gave her shoulder a comforting squeeze. "Don't tear yourself up over it. That whole situation was a mess. That whole family was a mess. We all knew it was just a disaster waiting to happen. Hell, Kate, we've had earthquakes that were less of a surprise than Lisa Getty's shooting."

"But now Chaney's dead. If I'd moved quicker, he might not be." She thought of the dead man the only time she'd seen him alive, his burned-out eyes exhausted in a face streaked with black makeup, his thin body tense beneath worn fatigues. "To have come all the way through the war, to have made it this far, and then to die like that."

"Your grandmother would say you were only trying to take care of your own."

Her head snapped up. "My grandmother would say a lot of things I wouldn't agree with. My grandmother would say a lot of things I would say were full of shit."

He left his hand on her shoulder, a warm and sympathetic presence. "Looks like people are going back in," he said after a while. "You coming?"

She roused herself and gave him a wan smile. "You bet I'm coming. This game's going into overtime. I wouldn't miss it for the world."

Mutt gave a long-suffering sigh and collapsed in a heap with her nose buried pointedly beneath her tail as Kate followed Bobby inside.

The second half was as hard fought as the first, with increasing fouls as each team tired and the final quarter ran out. With twenty seconds on the clock Eknaty Kvasnikof was fouled going in for a lay-up, and the ref called for a one-and one. Swish, swish, and the score at the buzzer was tied, 73–73. Overtime was quick and dirty and the Kanuyaq Kings took it, much to the delight of the hometown crowd, which got to its feet and cheered both

teams impartially, and indeed seemed reluctant to leave the gym at all.

As his victorious team trotted off the floor with much less energy than they had shown trotting on, Bernie looked up and found Kate in the stands. He held up five fingers and pointed at the door. She nodded and slipped outside.

People were standing around in excited groups, shivering in the now cold night air but reluctant to bring the evening to an close. Proud parents reenacted particularly brilliant plays made by their offspring, built up Seldovia's defensive capabilities so that it was a miracle of talent and guts every time Niniltna scored, and argued heatedly over each and every referee call. Kate saw money change hands more than a few times.

"Kate." She turned to find Bernie with Eknaty Kvasnikof, the latter bundled in sweats. The coach hovered protectively over his player, reminding Kate of nothing so much as a mother duck shepherding her duckling across a pond.

There was a tendency on the part of the crowd to muscle in next to Eknaty. Kate signaled to Mutt. Mutt rose and stretched and stalked purposefully between Kate, Bernie and Eknaty and everyone else on the school grounds. Everyone else on the school grounds halted their forward motion. Mutt didn't bark, she didn't even growl, she just grinned at them, her tongue lolling out between two rows of extremely large and pointed teeth, as Kate and Bernie and Eknaty disappeared around a corner.

They found some privacy between the school's utility outbuilding and a World War II Quonset hut that served as the administrative annex. "Bernie tell you why I wanted to talk to you?" she asked the boy.

He was tall and slender, with smooth skin and troubled brown eyes. His straight brown hair fell over his forehead, and brushing it back was a nervous habit. He nodded without looking at her.

"Were you at Lisa and Lottie's that morning? The morning Lisa was shot?"

He nodded again.

"What time?" He said nothing, and she said, "Eknaty, what time were you there?"

He remained silent. Kate looked at Bernie. Bernie said, "Natty."

That was all, but the word of a boy's basketball coach carries a weight with that boy that will not be denied. "Early," the boy said, mumbling the single word.

"How early?"

He swallowed, his Adam's apple bouncing. "Lottie wanted me there at sunrise. I got there a little late, around seven."

"To do what?"

He shrugged, hands dug in his pockets, kicking at the snow. "Whatever needed doing. Chop wood, do the spring service on the tractor. She said something about scraping the hull on the boat, too. She was going to tell me what to do, but she wasn't there when I got there." He flushed painfully, and in the harsh, pitiless glare of the school's outdoor lights Kate saw that his eyes were filling up with tears.

Suddenly, she knew. "Lisa was there, though, wasn't she?" she asked him.

He hesitated, then nodded.

Kate's eyes met Bernie's. She gave her head a tiny, significant jerk. His brows drew together and he opened his mouth as if to protest. Something in her set, stern face dissuaded him. He hesitated, looked from her to the boy, and moved out of earshot.

A quick look around satisfied her that no one had discovered them, and in a low voice Kate said, "Okay, Eknaty. What did she do?"

He dug the toe of his sneaker into the snow. "Nothing."

"Eknaty, somebody shot her—"

"I didn't!"

"I know you didn't," Kate said soothingly, "but some-body did, and I've got to find out who, and that means I need to know everything about her. Talk to me. What did Lisa do that day?"

He looked hard at the blue tin side of the gym. "One of the things Lottie told me she wanted me to do was haul their winter's trash to the dump. I'd been working at it for an hour, hour and a half, and I was bagging it up in the backyard when Lisa came out. She—" He stopped, his face scarlet.

But Kate knew. "Did she touch you?" He nodded. "Kiss you?" He nodded again. "Maybe more than that? Maybe make love to you?"

"It wasn't making love," Eknaty said in an agonized voice. There was a brief, pain-filled pause, and then the words seemed to burst forth, tumbling one over the other, as if the story had been dammed up for too long behind a barrier of shame and embarrassment and the overwhelming uncertainty and awkwardness of adolescence. "When I touch Betty"—Kate identified Betty as Betty Moonin, one of her cousins on her mother's side, a plump, sweet-faced girl of sixteen—"it feels good. Lisa was like . . . she was like an animal, like . . . like a dog dragging its butt on the ground when it comes in heat. She smelled funny, like, I don't know, almost sour, but sweet, too, only too sweet. She kept touching me, all over. I . . . I didn't want to, but she kept touching me, all over, and I . . ."

"Ssshh," Kate said, stemming the flow of near hysteria with a soothing voice. She didn't make the mistake of forcing another unwanted embrace on the boy. "Ssshh, now, Natty. It's all right now."

"No, it's *not*," he flared, wiping tears away with a clumsy hand. "I hated it, but I couldn't stop doing it. I know they say teenagers never think about anything else, but I really didn't want to. But I couldn't tell her no. She

wanted me and she made me want her. I thought I was going to . . . I had to go along. I couldn't stop it."

He hung his head. Kate saw another tear slip down his cheek and suddenly felt very old. There were a number of things she could have said then. She could have pointed out how a seventeen-year-old boy was more in the charge of his hormones than of his head. She could have explained how much distance there was between having sex and making love. She could have run down the notches on Lisa Getty's bedpost for him.

She waited until he'd regained some of his composure. "Eknaty," she said, "somebody shot her. Somebody looked down the barrel of a 30.06 and sighted in on her the way you or I would a moose. Somebody pulled the trigger, knowing they were aiming at a person, a human being." She raised her hand, pointing to her bandage. "When I started trying to find out who, they took a shot at me." He looked up, startled out of his misery. She nodded. "I was lucky. Max Chaney, the new ranger, wasn't. They found his body this afternoon." He sucked in a breath. His face, already bleached out in the merciless glow of the electric lights, went white to the lips. "We have to find out who did it, Eknaty, all of it. We have to make sure they never do it again."

His head bent. She waited. When he raised it again, the shame had not altogether faded from his features but at least now he didn't look as if he would crumple at a harsh word. "She took me . . . we were in the barn," he said, steadily enough. "Then we heard the shots. Lottie came around the cabin." He flinched. "She saw us coming out of the barn," he said painfully. "She could tell what we . . . what we . . . well, she didn't say anything, but you could tell what she was thinking." He swallowed. "Lisa laughed at her. I was watching Lottie, and for a second I thought . . ."

"What? What did you think?"

He took a deep breath and said, "For a second I thought Lottie was going to hit her." He shook his head. "You know how big Lottie is? Well, when she's mad, she looks about twice that big. She looks . . . she looks as big as a grizzly. Only more scary." Kate didn't laugh, and he shivered. "Lisa didn't even back up. She just kept looking at Lottie, like, like . . ."

"Like what?"

"Like Lottie wasn't her sister at all, like Lottie was this, like, joke she lived with, and had to put up with, but one she didn't have to pay any attention to, or . . . or respect. You know? It was like in Lisa's world, Lottie didn't count." He looked up at Kate, his young face sick. "She even nudged me and winked at me when Lottie was yelling at her, like I was supposed to laugh at Lottie, too."

"Did you?"

"No." He shook his head back and forth violently. "No way Jose. Lottie must outweigh me by seventy-five pounds, and she was mad enough. Besides . . ."

"Besides what?"

He smiled, a brief, weak, sad little smile Kate's heart ached to see. "I always liked Lottie. When she went on a hunt with Uncle Chick and me one time, up back of the Tellglliqs, she taught me how to shoot, with her own rifle. I was just a kid, and Uncle Chick had a bottle along for company. She was pretty disgusted with him, so she took me out alone the next day. She helped me get my first caribou. I guess she felt sorry for me or something because after that she let me go fishing with her, and even bear hunting one time. She always hires me on for odd jobs around their place every spring. She doesn't talk much, but she's always nice to me. I like her," he repeated.

Kate waited patiently until he finished. "But, on that morning . . ."

He shivered. "I'd never seen Lottie mad before. When she finished yelling at Lisa, she told us about finding Steve Syms's body at his house."

"Why had she gone there?"

"She was going to hire him to help scrape the hull on the bowpicker so we could copper paint it. Anyway, when she stopped yelling at Lisa, she went back in the house and came out with their parkas and rifles and threw Lisa's at her. And then she went to the garage and—"

"They each had their own rifle?"

He looked over at her, surprised at the question. "Sure, Kate. They always each took their own. Sometimes I thought Lottie'd had hers welded to her shoulder."

"Eknaty, are you sure? You remember seeing Lisa and Lottie each with their own rifle?"

He looked bewildered. "Yes. I'm sure. Lottie had her new rifle, the one Max gave her for her birthday. They were still going together then."

"What!" The exclamation was forced out of Kate.

He jumped and looked at her, and she forced her voice down. "Max and Lottie were going together?"

"Sure. Didn't you know? Max met Lottie first. He even went sheep hunting with us last November."

Kate, feeling as if the world were shaking a little beneath her feet, was barely able to restrain her incredulity. "Were they . . . did they . . . was it . . . romantic?" she said finally.

He blushed and ducked his head. "He slept with her in her tent."

Kate sighed, a long, deep sigh. "I guess that's romantic enough."

At that moment a hovering Bernie swooped down and rescued Eknaty from Kate's fell clutch, offering a blanket curse on her offspring if Eknaty's performance the following day was less than perfect. "Always supposing some misguided fool feels inclined to beget offspring

upon you," he added acidly, herding Eknaty before him.

"Right, thanks, Bernie," she replied in an abstracted voice. He paused for a moment and watched her walk away, his forehead puckered, before shaking himself and trotting off after Eknaty. There was a postgame analysis to be held, weaknesses in offense and defense to be identified, a dozen teenagers flushed with success to be tucked safely into bed, and two more days of games to plan for. Bernie had no time to waste on mere murder.

nine

THE next morning George Perry roared up to Bobby's house on a Skidoo and off-loaded a grim-faced Jack. He entered without knocking, stamping the snow off his feet, and demanded, "Why didn't you wait for me up on the Step?"

Kate looked over at him coolly. "I had to talk to someone."

Jack counted to ten. "Okay," he said. "They shipped the body out to Anchorage last night. Forensics promised to have the bullet out and run a ballistics test on it by this morning, and Chopper Jim'll get the news to us as soon as they do."

"Thirty-ought-six?" Bobby asked.

"Looks like. Won't know for sure until ballistics gets the slug."

"It won't be the same rifle," Kate said.

Jack's head whipped around. "What?"

"The bullet didn't come from the same rifle that killed Lisa Getty."

"How do you know that?" he demanded.

"There were too many people in the area. After shooting Lisa, the killer had to ditch the rifle in the woods, or be caught with it. Chaney was shot with a different rifle."

"If the killer dumped the rifle that shot Lisa Getty in those woods, where is it? I've had twenty officers and investigators beat feet over every inch of those goddam

161

woods at least five times apiece. Where the hell is it?"

"It's there." Forestalling, she knew for the moment only, further questions on the subject, she treated him to an abridged version of her last two days' activities. "You have been a busy girl," he said at last, frowning. "So what'd you do with the bear bladders and the tusks?" He looked at her blank face. "Don't tell me you left them on the boat?"

"How dumb do you think I am?"

"Don't tempt me. So what did you do with them?"

"I sold them."

Jack's jaw dropped. "What!"

Kate shrugged. "I found a buyer who wanted them. He had cash."

"Jesus, Kate!"

"How much did you get?" Bobby said.

"Sixty-six hundred."

"Jesus Christ, Kate!"

Bobby gave a long, low, respectful whistle. "For half a dozen bladders, that's eleven hundred apiece. Not bad, Kate. Not bad at all."

"I thought so, too," she said with a trace of pride.

"Sweet Jesus!" Jack said, varying his reaction.

"Bear's private parts come high these days," Bobby observed.

"I know," she said, her smile fading. "Dan's already worried about the poaching going on in the Park. If the price goes up any more, the Park Service is going to have to hire a bodyguard for every black bear in it."

"Sweet Jesus H. Christ on a *crutch!*"

"What's your problem?" Kate asked Jack, annoyed and a little hurt. "You think I shouldn't have sold them? Why? The bears were dead, Lisa's dead, and I needed the cash. You know how far sixty-six hundred dollars can take me? I'll be able to fish for myself this year, instead of guiding some jackass Outsider who can't figure out why

his ten-pound test keeps breaking every time he snags a Kanuyaq king."

Bobby eyed the fists gripping the arms of Jack's chair and hoped the chair would hold up under the strain. "Kate," Jack said with great calm, "by selling those bladders you have violated the Endangered Species Act, on top of which you can be charged with smuggling, shooting out of season, shooting over your limit, and God knows what else."

She smiled at him. "Prove it. And I didn't shoot them. Lisa did."

"Jesus!" Jack said, his momentary calm deserting him. "If Dan O'Brian ever finds out!" His face changed color, and he said in a hollow voice, "Jesus! Those bladders were evidence in an ongoing murder investigation. If Chopper Jim ever finds out, he'll throw us all in jail!"

"You plan on telling them?" Kate inquired. "Either one of them?"

Jack's voice deserted him, and he stared at her, speechless. "I suppose you sold him the walrus tusks, too?" he asked finally, if his expression was any indication, without much hope.

Kate was shocked and more than a little indignant. "Certainly not! What the hell kind of person do you think I am ?"

"I'd answer that truthfully, but I like living," Jack told Bobby. "What's the difference between taking the bear bladders and taking the tusks?"

Still indignant, Kate snapped, "The difference is you can't give the bladders back to the bears."

"Oh? And you can give the tusks back to the walrus?"

"No, I can't give the tusks back to the walrus," Kate said, aping Jack's heavily sarcastic tone, "but I can and will pass them on to Chick Noyukpuk, and he can carve them into cribbage boards or sea otters or *anua* for spirit masks and sell them to an Anchorage gift shop and maybe

make a few bucks. That way, the tusks stay where they're supposed to, in the Park, or at least whatever Chick earns from them will. The bladders would just get tossed in the trash."

"Chick Noyukpuk? The Billiken Bullet? The drunk musher who wrecks every snow machine he sets eye on?" Jack threw up his hands and addressed the ceiling. "Oh well, then how could I possibly object?"

"When he's sober he is a fine artist," Kate snapped.

"Time!" Bobby roared. "Much as I approve of comic relief, you two are worse than a couple of kids. Food's on, shut up, sit down, and eat. Now!" he roared, when Jack opened his mouth.

Kate and Jack sat. The food, an omelet seasoned with caribou sausage and sharp cheddar, was delicious, which was a good thing, since conversation lagged.

Kate was clearing the table when a distant whap-whap-whap heralded the arrival of the trooper. The engine grew louder, settled and died. Heavy footsteps crunched the ice created by the overnight drop in temperature, followed by a perfunctory thump on the door before it opened. Chopper Jim stepped inside.

"Hey, Jim," Bobby said.

"Bobby," the trooper replied. "Jack. Kate."

"Had your breakfast?"

"Yeah. I wouldn't say no to a cup of coffee, though."

"Coming right up."

They arranged themselves around the fireplace and waited until Bobby had handed out steaming mugs. "Well?" Jack said.

"It's a match," Jim said.

Kate's head jerked up and Jack smirked at her.

Jim fished something small out of a breast pocket and tossed it to Kate. She caught it automatically, a misshapen slug of lead. She looked from it to Jack in sudden suspicion, and he nodded. "When I left the Step I went down to the boat. I dug it out of the forward

bulkhead of the cabin." He smiled thinly. "It looks worse than your head."

Kate turned to Jim. "This match the bullet that killed Max Chaney?"

He nodded.

"But not the bullet that killed Lisa Getty." Her voice was certain and Jack looked annoyed.

Chopper Jim shook his head. "Nope."

The single, laconic syllable irritated her. "Lisa Getty was growing commercial quantities of marijuana in her backyard, Jim," she said. "Why didn't you mention that when you talked to Jack?"

"I didn't know."

"Come on!" Kate glared at him. "Lisa had enough pot in that greenhouse to put the entire Park into orbit without benefit of rocket. I found drying frames and a case of baggies in the barns. No one knows his beat better than a small town cop, and in people this Park is just one gigantic small town. If anybody knew that Lisa was growing dope, you would."

He looked at her, at her angry face, a meditative expression on his own. "We didn't talk much."

"You didn't have to, talk to *her,* anyway," she retorted. "You knew, didn't you? Probably about the dealings in walrus ivory and bear bladders and sealskins and sea otter hides—hell, Lisa probably shot sea gulls, just for the hell of it! Why didn't you tell Jack?"

"Kate," Bobby said.

"I'll tell you why," Kate said, ignoring Bobby. "Because you wanted me to do your dirty work for you. Because you didn't want to piss off everyone in the Park following up leads that led, for one reason or another, into just about every house and cabin and cache in a million square acres! Not to mention which half the men in the Park went into mourning when she died. That's no secret, in fact, for my purpose it's probably better to assume she's slept with everyone I've talked

to so far. Including you," she said pointedly. She looked at the trooper, raised an eyebrow and added, "And just where were you the morning Lisa Getty got shot?" She brightened a little. "Where were you when Max Chaney got shot?"

Bobby turned a sharp laugh into a choking fit, and even Jack had to smile. "What about you?" Chopper Jim asked, affable and unperturbed. "Where was I when somebody took a shot at you, Kate?"

"Kate," Bobby said again, and something in his firm, inexorable tone halted her in mid-tirade. "All this is beside the point and you know it. Get to it, woman."

He was right, and Kate stopped dancing around and got to it. "I know where the rifle that killed Lisa Getty is."

"What?" The three men spoke with one voice.

"You didn't tell me that yesterday," Bobby snapped.

"I didn't realize where it was until last night, and we couldn't have found it in the dark."

"And you can today? This morning?"

"I think so."

"Need any help?" Chopper Jim asked with a guileless expression.

"You've been such a big help so far, working so hard, doing so much legwork, sharing information on this case, I think we can allow you a little time off now," Kate cooed.

She was incensed when he didn't bother to look offended. He drained his mug and rose to his feet. "Then I'll be off." He put on his hat and touched a finger to its brim. "Anything I can do."

Kate thought of several things he could do, none of them productive of results in a murder investigation but all of them deeply satisfying to contemplate. He knew it, and from the hint of the smile on his face she knew he knew it. She waited until the door closed behind him,

but not long enough for him to be out of earshot. "Prick," she said, with heartfelt loathing.

The sound from the porch might have been a cough or a laugh, and Kate sat, stewing, until the sound of the chopper died away, and then said to Jack, "Suit up. Mutt, up and at 'em. Let's move like we got a purpose, people."

She sounded just like the drill instructor Bobby had had at San Diego. He removed himself from the line of fire, stayed there until the door closed behind them and gave a loud, vociferous sigh of relief that he was staying home.

"We've been over this ground, the troopers have been over this ground, everybody in Niniltna has been over this ground a hundred times. The troopers bagged enough crap to top off the Anchorage landfill. Why are we back here?" Jack's voice was plaintive.

"I still can't believe it took me so long to figure out," she said, and followed the yellow crime-scene tape, tattered now but still showing a ragged path through the trees, walking in the reconstructed path of the killer. When she came to where Lisa's body had lain, Kate halted for a moment, the memory of yesterday's witches' coven shivering through her. Determinedly, she shook it off and reached for the nearest birch and, hand over hand, pulled it down to the ground until it bowed into a U-shape. She examined its top carefully and let it spring back. She reached for the birch beside it.

Jack watched her, mystified. "What in the hell are you doing?"

Kate nodded at the next clump of birches. "Start pulling those down."

"What!"

"Pull down the goddam trees and look at their tops," Kate half shouted, her ruined voice a rough scrape across exposed nerves.

"All right, all right, anything for a quiet life." Jack waded through the snow to the nearest tree and yanked its trunk into a taut, straining bow.

"Careful," Kate snapped, "don't break them, just bend them so you can see their tops."

"What, there aren't enough of them around, you're afraid I'll injure one beyond all hope of recovery and eternally upset the ecological balance of the Park?"

Stepping back, she released the hold she had on her birch and let it spring upright. Its top whipped past his face and vaulted erect to some twenty-five feet above their heads. Kate watched it weave back and forth in a steadily slackening swing, among a thickly clustered group of birches huddling together in insular fraternity, keeping all their cards close to their white, birch-bark chests, all secrets secluded within the tops of their rustling branches.

"Wait a minute," she said. She smacked her forehead in irritation. "Where is my head at? She'd have tied it off to a spruce, or a birch next to a spruce, in a clump of them probably. Yeah, for better concealment until the leaves came out."

Her grin was tight. "It's the same problem I've been having all along, not seeing the trees for the forest." Stepping back, she surveyed the scene through narrowed eyes. "Here. I'll try this one. You start on that clump over there."

He shook his head, wrestling with his scrub spruce. "Kate, you have had me doing some pretty dumb things in my life, but this—" His voice died away, as he stared at the top of the tree he had pulled down.

The 30.06 was tied lengthwise to the topmost part of the trunk of a tall, slender spruce. The butt rested in the crotch where a branch met the trunk; lengths of green fishing twine, the kind used for net mending, bound the stock and barrel tightly to the bark. The stock was sticky with pine sap.

Kate slogged through the wet, shifting snow to reach around him. The twine was damp and crusted with sap as well, and after a few moments' tugging, Kate pulled her knife and cut it. Jack uttered an inarticulate protest about destroying evidence. She stilled it with a single shake of her head. "We won't need it."

He let the tree go and stood staring at her through narrowed eyes as it swung back and forth above them in steadily diminishing arcs. "You know who did it, don't you."

It wasn't a question, and she didn't answer.

"You find it?" Bobby asked the moment they walked in.

Kate nodded curtly. Mutt squatted next to the door, ears up, watching Kate's every move with an intent yellow gaze.

"You find her?"

"Her who?" Jack inquired.

"Didn't look."

"Why not?"

"I already know where she is."

"Where?"

Kate jerked a thumb over her shoulder. "George hired her to take a climbing party up the Big Bump."

"Going up Angqaq Peak, eh?" Bobby shook his head. "Beats me why some people go to all that trouble just because it's there. Me, I'll settle for the Discovery Channel." He cocked his head, eyeing her with a bright, inquisitive gaze, looking like an black-eyed, black-headed robin. "She really do it?"

Kate nodded her head at the pillar of electronics that held up the center of the house. "Can you raise the Park on that thing?"

Bobby was hurt. "I can raise Tranquility Base on that thing if I have to. Who you want to talk to?"

"Dan O'Brian."

"Consider it done," Bobby said grandly and rolled to the radio.

Kate's conversation with Dan O'Brian was short and terse. Jack's lips set in a thin line as he listened. Bobby signed off when she was through, and Kate looked around from the radio. "Where's your pack?"

"In the closet in the corner. You going after her?"

Kate opened the closet door, and like the Kanuyaq when the ice melted, its contents cascaded onto the floor in a fierce, joyous current of junk. She waded through it and pulled out an old canvas pack on a metal frame. "Got any longies?"

"Left-hand drawer under the bed, right side. Where'd you find the rifle?"

She found the long underwear and began to strip, as Bobby looked on, frankly admiring, and as Jack looked on, angry at both of them but smart enough to hide it, or try to. "I'm so slow I make glacial erosion look speedy," Kate said, voice muffled in her sweater. She fumbled for the right holes in the longie top and shoved her hands through. "I was standing there looking at those trees, and I *knew* it had to be there somewhere. It had to be. Then last night, when I was talking to Eknaty and he was telling me about when Lottie took him hunting, I remembered how Abel taught me to keep game out of the reach of bear and wolves and wolverines while we he were on a hunt. You got some wool socks?" This as she donned jeans over the longies.

He watched until the last inch of skin was covered, and then, with a sigh of regret for all good things past, Bobby said, "I don't have any feet, Kate."

"Right, sorry, I forgot." She looked at Jack, who sat down and began unlacing his boots.

"Find yourself a nice, young, supple, medium-sized birch," Kate continued. "Bend it down, stake it out, tie your meat or your supplies or whatever you want to keep out of the reach of whoever or whatever walks below

while you're gone, and let it go. Simple, effective. I don't know why it is, but nobody ever looks up. You got a vest?"

"Eddie Bauer one-hundred percent pure goose down." Kate smiled slightly. "Only the best."

"You bet." He rolled over to the coatrack, snagged the vest and tossed it to her. "You tie something as bulky as a rifle to the top of a birch tree with no leaves on it, somebody's going to see it eventually."

She pulled on the vest and snapped it closed. "Then you pick a spruce, one young enough to bend but old enough to have some height. Pick one in a clump of birch and spruce and cottonwood, all tangled up together, on a piece of state land anybody would be instantly jailed for trying to clear, and if you do it right you couldn't see it from the air, let alone the ground."

Bobby shook his head. "Lot of traffic around there, air and ground. Sounds iffy to me."

"She was in a hurry." Kate shrugged. "It's hard to quarrel with success. Even I had a hard time figuring out what she did with it, and I've known Lottie all my life."

Jack was rummaging in his grip for spare socks. At Kate's words, he paused, his thick eyebrows coming together in a frown. "You knew."

"Knew what?" Kate held up a pair of glove liners and paused, looking down at the pack.

"You know who did it. You've always known."

"Oh for crying out loud, Jack," she said, exasperated. "What's the matter with you? What's the first thing you taught me on the job? What's Morgan's First Law? 'The nearest and the dearest got the motive with the mostest.' Of course I knew. I doubt that there was a soul in the Park, who thought about it for more than thirty straight seconds, who *didn't* know who did it."

"Really," Jack said between his teeth. "Mind telling me how?"

She looked down at the glove liners, looked up at Bobby. "Take 'em," he said. "Better to have 'em and not need 'em than the alternative."

She checked her watch. "We've got just enough time for a bedtime story. I'm only going to tell it once, so listen carefully.

"Once upon a time, there was a man and a wife living in the Alaskan bush. They had two daughters. The oldest was a bear of a child, something over ten pounds at birth, and from the time she could walk and talk she was a taciturn, difficult person. I don't think she ever was a girl." Kate paused. "Although I'm not sure she ever was a woman, either."

Jack wanted to ask what the hell that meant, but Kate went on. "The younger daughter, born ten years later, was everything the elder was not. She was little, she was dainty, she was pretty, she was charming. She had all the social graces Lottie lacked."

Kate smiled. It was not a nice smile. "Naturally, her parents, in particular her father, who disapproved of unfemininity on male chauvinist principals, just loved Lisa to death."

"And Lottie?"

"Oh, he tolerated Lottie. They both did. They put up with her. They were aware of their responsibilities as her parents, after all." Jack flinched at the sarcasm in her voice. "At least her mother was. Her father ridiculed her, which just confirmed her sense of worthlessness. She became morbidly sensitive over her size—"

"I've met her," Jack said in a puzzled voice. "She's not that big." He tossed Kate the spare socks he'd pulled from his daypack.

She caught them. "Thanks. Next to you, no. Next to Lisa? And she was next to Lisa every day of her life."

Jack nodded slowly.

"Well. Lottie never behaved quote, normally, unquote. She was defensive, antagonistic and so hard to get along

with that her family not unnaturally turned with immense relief to Lisa, who responded to the attention by getting better grades, going on to college and then choosing to return home to live. What about a tent?" she said to Bobby. "Just in case?"

"There's my survival kit."

"Perfect."

"You be careful with it, woman. I just bought it new." He hauled at a bundle of what looked like fabric and short sticks in a fluorescent orange stuff bag. Another stuff bag appeared, this one with a sleeping bag and a rolled foam pad inside it.

Kate strapped the bags to the bottom of the backpack as Bobby rolled into the kitchen and ransacked the cupboards for his camp cooking gear. "In all that time, Lottie, who I don't think ever left the Park—"

"Heads up."

She looked up just in time to field the cooking kit, and tucked it into a side pocket. Bobby piled a dozen foil packages of prepackaged food in his lap and wheeled them over.

"Well, Lottie had no life except what was lived in Lisa's shadow. Then along came Max Chaney, who for reasons unknown takes it into his head to fall in love with Lottie."

"What!" Even Bobby was staring at her.

"Eknaty Kvasnikof was working for Lottie part-time. He says they had something going." She shook her head. "They say there's someone for everybody. Maybe Max was for Lottie. But . . ." She looked at Jack and grinned, a narrow, unamused little grin. "You knew this was coming, right? Lisa seduces Max away. Lottie befriends Eknaty Kvasnikof, and Lisa seduces him, too. Lisa puts their livelihood at risk shooting black bears for their bladders and walrus for their tusks and growing pot in felonious quantities and God knows what else. She puts every social relationship, every friend of the

family at risk by screwing anything in the Park on two legs. You got any chocolate, Bobby?"

Bobby looked offended. "It's one of the four major food groups, right? Of course I have something with chocolate in it. You want gorp?"

"All you got."

"Hershey bars?"

Her head snapped up, and she looked at him hopefully. "I can go farther on a Hershey bar than I can on a porterhouse steak. You got some?"

He produced half a box from the freezer like a magician producing a rabbit from a hat.

"Meanwhile, back at the Tale of Two Sisters," Jack prodded impatiently.

Kate tucked the chocolate carefully into another pocket on the pack. "You know, Jack, if you treat someone like shit for long enough, pretty soon they're going to start looking around for the bottom of a shoe to scrape themselves off of. The reverse," she added, "holds true. If you treat someone like a saint for long enough, pretty soon they start believing their shit don't stink. That was Lisa all over. She could do no wrong. All you had to do was ask her.

"I'm sure Lottie protested Lisa's behavior. I'm equally certain Lisa ignored those protests, when she didn't laugh them off. After everything I've heard this past week, I wouldn't put it past Lisa to have deliberately looked around for more and better ways to piss Lottie off. She enjoyed it." Kate reached for Jack's spare socks. She donned them on top of her own and the ones he'd taken off, and her feet barely fit back into her own boots. She shook her head, removed one pair, put her boots back on, and pulled the last pair of socks on over her boots. "It's been a way of life," she said, "for both of them. All the ego Lottie lost, Lisa got." She rose to her feet and took a few investigatory steps. Her boots felt snug but not tight. The wool of the socks stretched over the

soles of her boots squeaked against the hardwood floor. "Hardly any of this was news, to me or to anyone else who's lived in the Park for the last twenty years."

She looked at Jack. "Yes, in answer to your question, I did know who killed Lisa Getty, almost from the first moment of being told she had not been killed by Roger McAniff. I defy you to find someone in the Park who didn't."

Jack whipped his head around to stare accusingly at Bobby. "It was pretty obvious," Bobby admitted.

"You got a ski pole or something, Bobby?"

"Right, Kate, I do so much skiing. How about a broom handle?"

"If that's what you got, that's what I'll take."

Reaching in back of the refrigerator, Bobby pulled out a broom and sawed off the handle with a serrated steak knife.

Jack felt left out. Bobby and Kate seemed to understand all, he nothing. He paced off a length, turned and bellowed, "Mind telling me why the hell we've spent all this time running our asses off over a billion square acres of wilderness trying to find some other poor schmuck who might have killed her?"

"Lottie's dying, anyway." Kate looked up and met Jack's eyes and insisted, "Yes, spiritually, she is. She's lost her foil." Her voice was sad. "What happens when you look in the mirror and nothing looks back? She doesn't have anyone left to hate, and I think hate is all that kept her going. Except maybe for those few weeks when she and Max Chaney were an item. But Max Chaney was only a man. Lisa was her *sister*. Men might come and men might go, but for better or worse, Lisa was her sister."

Kate looked up at Jack. "You bet I looked for somebody else. I wanted a hundred other somebodies to point at and say maybe. I didn't want to have to put Lottie in jail, and I didn't think she was a danger to anyone else."

"She took a shot at you!"

"Yes," Kate admitted. "But if she'd really wanted to kill me, she would have. Lottie hits what she aims at."

"Like Martin," Bobby said.

"Yes," Kate said, almost wry, "in the last six months I've had more than my share of people shooting at me without meaning to get a hit."

"You've got to get into a different line of work," Bobby agreed.

"Will you two stop making like Stan and Ollie and get serious!"

"She did shoot Max Chaney, before you could talk to him," Bobby pointed out.

"Yes." Kate nodded, her smile fading. "Yes, Max Chaney is dead. Lottie must have known it was only a matter of time before I found out she'd been seeing him."

"You think he knew?"

"I don't know." Kate shook her head. "I didn't know him. And now he's dead, and that is my fault."

"You didn't pull the trigger."

"I could have stopped her. I should have. I didn't." The sound of a distant helicopter crept in beneath the door. She shrugged into her parka, donned glove liners and gloves and hoisted the pack to her back. "Now I have to, before she hurts someone else."

"Which way you going?" Bobby asked her.

"Which way does Lottie usually take her climbing parties?"

"Jesus, Kate. You could always wait for her to come down."

"I'm not sure she's coming down. She knows I know the truth. I as good as told her so in the woods yesterday. She'll know that by now I've found out about Chaney. No." Kate shook her head. "I don't think she's coming down. Not the way she went up, anyway. The Canadian border's on the other side of the Big Bump, remem-

ber, along with about two hundred thousand square miles of Yukon Territory. She gets that far, we'll never find her."

"Be careful," Bobby said. "Be awful goddam careful, Kate."

"I'm always careful, Bobby. Sometimes I'm not very smart, but I'm always careful."

Mutt was on her feet, tail curled tightly over her rump. The noise of the approaching helicopter increased as the door opened. Through it the two men could see a Llama touching lightly down in the center of the clearing, Dan O'Brian in a headset on the stick. Kate ducked her head and ran toward it.

Jack said, "So which way is she going?"

Bobby, an unaccustomed expression of worry on his broad face, said, "Up the Valley of Death."

"And just what the *fuck* is the Valley of Death?"

"It's a glacial valley leading up the southwest face of Angqaq Peak." Bobby saw Jack's expression and elaborated. "It's a chronic avalanche trap. Hence the name. Climbers hate it, but it's the best approach for the Bump."

"Great." Jack started for the door, barefooted.

Bobby's voice halted him before he'd gone one step. "Do you know how to climb mountains?"

Jack turned, and Bobby said, "Kate does. You'd just get in her way."

Jack stared at him, impotent and enraged. He didn't have any real qualms about slugging a guy in a wheelchair, but Bobby was a friend. He swung around and, lacking a better target, put his fist through the wall next to the door.

"It's hell when us macho hero types have to let the heroine rescue herself, ain't it?" Bobby said sympathetically. He turned his chair and said over his shoulder, "There's tools and some Sheetrock in the workshop, when you get around to fixing that wall."

• • •

She came up over the lip of Kantishna Caldera, the hollowed-out cone of an extinct volcano, and was reminded of the old Thunderbird myth, the giant birds who caught up whales in their claws and carried them off to the young waiting in their volcanic nests. No beat of giant wings stirred the cold, still air this afternoon, which burned into her lungs with every inhalation. Mutt paced next to her, her big pads leaving clear prints in the new powder. Mutt had been reluctant to get on the chopper, glum in getting off it and less than enthusiastic about the whole idea. She looked up at Kate. Are we having fun yet?

"Sure," Kate told her, and Mutt's gloomy expression said that she was glad one of them thought so.

Above them the Quilak Mountains clawed at the surface of the pale blue dome of the sky, and on every side they were confronted by the rough and tumble detritus left by the last remaining scions of the Ice Age. Talons of glaciers tore at the bosom of the earth, raking furrows of discontent in their attempt to deny their own recession, leaving behind jagged peaks covered with ice, narrow valleys filled with snow, and mounds of terminal moraine a thousand feet high.

There was nothing benevolent or welcoming about the Quilak Mountains. Kate felt that they were daring her in, that the temerity of her very presence in their midst was her acceptance of that dare. Puffing, she paused to check the southern horizon. She saw not even a hint of a trace of a wisp of a cloud, for which she devoutly thanked the weather gods. She faced forward again, the snow crunching beneath her feet, and reached the lip of the caldera in another ten strides.

Before her stretched the Valley of Death, a long narrow valley that from a distance looked like an enormous playground slide, cutting through surrounding ridges and cliffs to spill out over the foothills to the valley beneath.

Close up, she could see the overhanging snow cornices topping the vertical walls of rock and ice on either side, the smooth floor carved into crevasses a thousand feet long and forty feet wide, lying in wait for the unwary climber beneath masking drifts of deep snow. There were icy pillars of seracs, graveled, ridged eskers of glacial moraine, and erratics, huge boulders carried along and dropped haphazardly by glaciers long since melted and gone. It was a rough, dangerous path stretching up the south face of the mountain.

The mountain. Angqaq Peak. In Aleut, Big Peak. To mountaineers the world over, the Big Bump. Kate saw a wedge of land rearing up nineteen thousand feet and change, its pointed peak testing the boundaries of the sky. Its sides swept down, unbroken on the right, broken by one secondary peak on the left, similar in shape but two thousand feet less in height. The smaller peak sat at the right hand of Angqaq as if Angqaq was hand-rearing its own successor to take over the climber-killing business when Angqaq itself had retired. In fact climbers called the secondary peak "Child" and the primary peak "Mother," and, not infrequently, "you mother" and similar less than affectionate nicknames.

The rest of the Quilaks fell back before such terrible grandeur, their puny twelve- and fourteen- and sixteen-thousand-foot peaks as nothing next to *the* mountain. Taken collectively, their thrusting bulk was a challenge, a taunt, a provocation. Kate had been born next to the Quilaks and raised in the shadow of Angqaq, and still she was awed, and afraid.

Mutt uttered an impatient bark. Kate, startled back into her body, looked down. Mutt, blessed with no imagination and intimidated by nothing on the known planet, was all brisk business. We've done this before, she reminded Kate.

"Yes, we have," Kate said, sighing.

Well, then. Mutt broke into a trot and headed up the Valley of Death. Kate peered ahead, eyes narrowed against the glare of sun on snow even behind Bobby's Ray-Bans. She thought she saw a small, dark moving speck about halfway up the valley, but she couldn't be sure.

Only one way to find out. She adjusted the straps of her pack and fell in.

She toiled onward, up the long valley. Lost in the vast expanse of snow and ice, she trudged one step at a time, Mutt in the lead, which reminded her of the old joke about the view always being the same if you're not lead dog. She smiled, and the thought kept her going until she stumbled onto the remains of a campsite. A startled raven flew up, scolding her furiously.

"Ha, Trickster," she said, amused. "Caught you in the act."

She waved Mutt back and approached the camp cautiously. By the holes, she could see where they'd pitched their tent. A frozen round in the snow indicated the place someone had put down a hot pot. Going a little way from the site, she found a patch of yellow snow and evidence that Lottie's climbers had been eating too much, and she grimaced. They hadn't even buried their refuse, and if Kate hadn't been convinced of Lottie's state of mind before, she was now. The raven had ripped the remains of the camp apart. Kate sighed and shrugged out of her pack. Producing a collapsible shovel, she scooped the outdoor toilet into one of the empty food bags she found at the campsite.

"Pretty soon you're not going to be able to melt a drinkable pot of snow on this whole friggin' mountain," she muttered, and Mutt, nose wrinkled, gave an assenting sneeze. "At least you don't have to scoop it up," Kate told her.

She picked up the rest of the area, buried the trash against the Trickster's return and flagged the area for

later recovery. She paused, wondering if she were hungry. At thirteen thousand feet she had no desire for food or drink but knew it would be wise to force herself to have both. She choked down a chocolate bar and a couple of handfuls of gorp, managed to swallow half a quart of water, and marched on.

The higher she got, the worse her wound hurt. The sun beat down on her head, and she had to stop to remove her parka and gloves. Retaining glove liners, vest and knit hat, she stuffed everything else into her pack, hoisted it to her back and slogged on. On either side the walls of the valley rose a thousand feet straight up in a vertical wave of ice. The sun picked out the lines of the overhanging cornices, elaborately carved with an artisan's attention to detail by decades of wind blowing at gale force. Beyond the walls of the valley, the peaks of the Quilaks seemed to be closing in for the kill. After a while Kate tired of looking up and focused her attention strictly on the ground before her, which was a wise decision, since the floor of the Valley of Death was riddled with a thousand thousand crevasses, yawning chasms twelve and more feet deep where the glacial ice below had shifted and ruptured the surface. Some were hidden by deep snow, discovered only as she poked Bobby's broom handle in front of her. She was forced to double back half a dozen times. Progress was slow, and it was late afternoon when something out of the corner of her eye caught her attention. She looked up, and less than a mile in front of her three tiny figures leapt out from the vast expanse of whiteness. Two stood together, looking after a third who was double-timing up the valley at a gait perilously close to a trot.

Kate's heart pumped and she stepped out, rapidly closing the distance between herself and the two nearer figures. As she came up, they resolved into two young Oriental gentlemen, both of whom were dressed in top-of-the-line Everest chic and in spite of it looked very

cold. One of them rattled off a string of words at her, gesticulating excitedly and pointing after the retreating third figure.

"Do you speak English?" she asked them.

One of the Koreans said something, and it wasn't in English, so Kate said sternly, "Stay here. Don't move from this spot." She walked over to the nearest man and with both hands on his shoulders forced him down on his butt. "Stay *here,* or I'll . . ." She smiled, showing all her teeth, and drew a line across her throat with one finger. Her shirt collar parted and they could see her scar. Next to her, Mutt was smiling, too, and faced with Kate's scar and that gleaming expanse of enamel, the second Korean thumped down next to his comrade. Both nodded their heads vigorously, and Kate nodded back at them, satisfied. They'd been eating, and food wrappers littered the surrounding area. Kate picked up one, walked over to their packs—she was pleased to see them both shrink back as she passed by—and jammed it down the open mouth of the nearest one. She leveled a finger and said, her ruined voice rawer from the hike, "You pack it in, you pack it out. Got that?"

She didn't know if they had, but they both nodded in complete comprehension, nothing moving except their heads. One of them did give a little scream when she moved her knife around to a more comfortable place on her belt, but his friend patted him soothingly on the shoulder and he calmed. They blinked at her like two owls huddled together as she swung out of camp, following the single set of tracks that led due north, toward *the* mountain.

She was smaller than Lottie and she moved faster—she always had—and she gained on the distant figure rapidly. Soon she was close enough to hear Lottie breathing. The other woman must have known she was there, but she never turned, and Kate realized that she was heading steadily for the pass around the east summit, which

connected up on the Canadian side with the Slide, which was just that, one long slide east over the border.

Kate quickened her pace. Beneath her feet the ice cracked and the snow slid. She was panting with the exertion, sweating beneath her layers of clothes but not daring to take the time to stop and peel off another. The load shifted, and the pack thumped awkwardly against her spine. She staggered to one side, trying to regain her balance, but when a patch of ice exploded a foot in front of her boots she let the pack take her down, falling heavily on her left side. Mutt barked a warning and gathered her haunches beneath her. "No!" Kate said. "Stay!"

Flopping over, a flurry of shards from another patch of exploding ice told her Lottie was picking her shots carefully. She waited until her heart rate slowed down enough for her to speak. Cursing her ragged voice for its inability to carry, she squirmed over to a hummock of snow, wormed her way around it, Mutt squirming and worming beside her, inched forward toward another hummock and slid next to it in a third shower of exploding ice. Scared and angry, Kate yelled, "Dammit, Lottie, cut it out! You want to start an avalanche?"

There was no reply. "Come on, Lottie. You couldn't kill me before and I—"

"I sure as hell tried! If you hadn't tripped—"

"If I hadn't tripped you wouldn't have hit me at all!" Silence. "You're not going to kill me and you know it. Come on out. Come back down with me."

"I'll go to jail."

Kate was silent. It was true.

"Can you see me inside? In a cage? No air to breathe, no hills to walk, no hunting, no fishing, nothing? I might as well be dead."

"Lottie—"

"You know it's true, Kate. It's true of you, so you know it's true of me, too."

Kate's head drooped, until her forehead rested against the snow. Her hands dug into the ice on either side of her. "Why?" she said. "Why did you do it, Lottie? You must have known you'd be caught."

There was a pause, and when Lottie spoke again, Kate recoiled. The undertone of venom in the other woman's voice was a palpable force, spilling out in such an overwhelming wave that even this vast expanse of ice would not be enough to contain it, so fierce that the pain underlying it was almost indetectable. Almost. "I hated her, Kate. God, how I hated her. I think I hated her from the day she was born. I saw McAniff shoot that Jesus freak with a 30.06, and then I came home and saw her with Natty . . ."

Kate waited. When Lottie said no more, she called, "Lottie. I would have done everything I could to keep them from finding out it was you. Hell, the Park was lousy with people who believed with all their hearts that the world would be an infinitely better place if someone would just remove Lisa from it. I could have blown enough smoke to keep the cops feeling around blind until they gave up and went away." She paused, and then, the words wrung out of her, "Why, Lottie? Why did you have to kill Max? You might have gotten away with killing Lisa, but you knew I couldn't let you get away with killing Max."

Nothing. When Kate spoke again, her voice was sad. "When you asked me why he did it, you weren't talking about McAniff, were you? You were talking about Max. You were asking why he slept with Lisa, weren't you?" She waited. "Weren't you, Lottie?"

The silence was broken with a long, bestial cry, ripping across the frozen fabric of that mountain afternoon. Next to her Mutt howled in unison, and every hair on Kate's body stood straight up. The awful sound went on for what felt like forever, compounded of every hurt, every slight, every insult, every snide comment,

every smothered snicker, every cruel jibe, but mostly it was a lament for lost love—parental love, romantic love, maternal love. It was agony given voice.

Above all, it was a long, excruciating, mournful lament for the dead.

The sound broke off into a low sobbing, and left Kate limp and shaking. What could she say that could possibly get through that wall of anguish? Lottie's grief seemed so immense as to be a part of the earth itself.

The earth answered. Seventy miles beneath them, the North American continental plate rode over the top of the North Pacific oceanic plate, forcing it four and a quarter inches down into the earth's mantle. It was a bluntly struck blow of energy equal to slightly more than the atomic bomb exploded over Hiroshima. The primary shock, a single, hard, up-and-down jolt, knocked Kate, who was halfway to her feet, back to her knees. She fell forward, and the secondary shock, a continuing side-to-side motion, kept her from getting back up again. A layer of snow cascaded down over the hummock she crouched behind. Mutt, whimpering, flattened herself at Kate's side.

Echoing off the sky was the sound of a thousand gears grinding together as the entire valley shook back and forth, calling Kate to raise dazed, incredulous eyes and bear witness.

There was too much happening to take in at once. The broken, icy floor of the glacier undulated in the sinuous, deadly fashion of a serpent. The cornices of the glacier walls cracked, slipped and crashed to the bottom. The walls themselves broke apart and tumbled down in house-size chunks. Huge clouds of pulverized crystal billowed up into the still air, as if in a frenzy of spring cleaning a Titan had laid hold to the edge of the earth's mantle and with one snap of his wrists was shaking it free of a winter's accumulation of dust and debris.

A scream came from somewhere, a high, frightened, girlish scream. "Lottie!" Kate cried, but the name was torn from her mouth. She tried to stand, but her legs were like jelly and her feet wouldn't work. She gave up, wound a hand in Mutt's ruff and hung on.

Above the glacier the uneven reaches of the Quilaks jerked awake and surged to their feet. Miklluni Peak shrugged its shoulders, and before Kate's disbelieving eyes all one thousand feet of its west face slid down into one side of the valley. Opposite, Angqaq Peak shivered and shook, and from the East Buttress another avalanche raced down the opposite side of the glacial valley and met the oncoming one from Miklluni. They collided in the middle of the valley, and a white, mushroom-shaped cloud boiled up.

Everywhere she looked, every surface of snow was exploding into avalanches. Kate groveled before it all, crouched on hands and knees, one hand locked in Mutt's coat, the other clenched in the unstable floor of the Valley of Death.

Then, without warning, even that floor fell out from under her, yanking an involuntary scream from her throat, a sound of rough terror.

She was pulled up with a sharp jerk. Among the sounds of falling snow and grinding earth, it took a moment for her to realize that Mutt had caught her in her teeth, by the scruff of the neck as if she were a newborn pup. A grunt, a tug, and Kate was up over the edge of the new crevasse and spread-eagled on its side. Woman and dog, they lay there, trying to burrow into the unstable ground, riding out the rolling, quaking, shuddering upheaval of terra not so firma.

Seconds passed, minutes, Kate was sure hours had gone by. The shaking slowed, and stopped. The grinding sound ended. Slowly, painfully, Kate's world righted itself. She blinked, and the lens shifted from blur to sharp, clear focus. She became aware of the last rays

of the setting sun glinting off the ice, of the cold snow
beneath her cheek, of the constriction around her throat
where Mutt's jaws were locked into the back of her parka,
twisting the fabric into a noose of life. "Hey, loosen up
there, will you, girl?"

It took a few moments to talk Mutt into letting her go.
When she did at last, reluctantly, Kate raised her head
cautiously and looked around.

A new crevasse opened in front of her, falling straight
down in a path a hundred feet across. Perched on its edge,
she stared down into that blatant, leering boast of earthly
power that seemed to say, See? If I'd really wanted you,
I would have had you. Maybe next time you won't be so
lucky. The subterranean snicker was almost audible.

She rose to shaky feet and realized she no longer had
her pack. It must have been torn from her back during
the fall.

Next to her Mutt climbed to her feet and shook herself
vigorously, spraying Kate with ice and snow. She reared
to thrust a cold nose in Kate's face, as if to say, Can we
please get off this goddam mountain now?

Kate looked around apprehensively. "Not yet, girl.
Where's the pack?"

Mutt nosed out the pack some fifty feet away, teetering
on the edge of yet another entirely new chasm. Kate
pounced on the pack thankfully and cast an anxious
look around for shelter. A boulder-size chunk of ice
had been heaved up out of glacial bowels; it was all
she could find in the time she had left and it would
have to do. She dragged her pack over to its downhill
side and, not daring to look up the valley, emptied
it out. With still-shaking hands, she pitched her one-
man tent, anchored it down as best she could, shoved
the rest of her gear and Mutt inside and crawled in
behind them.

Mutt gave an anxious whine. "There's no time, girl.
Come on, move over."

The silence outside seemed to grow heavier with each passing moment, and its ominous threat made Kate's hands clumsy. She had barely gotten the tent zipped, the sleeping bag unrolled and herself inside it when the wave of spindrift from the collisions of the multiple avalanches hit like a blustery club. The thin Vortex walls of the tent flapped and strained, the weight of Kate and Mutt and the pack on the tent floor all that kept the wind from picking it up and rolling it end over end down the valley.

The wave of particulate ice pounded the tent for half an hour, a raging, howling force that screamed its frustration at not being able to get at them. The tent was sealed shut and still the inside was filled with tiny, whirling bits of ice. All Kate could do was lie there, draw as far back into the hood of Bobby's sleeping bag as she could get, and wait it out. She wondered if the avalanche would run out of steam before it got to her, but it seemed to be too much to worry about at the moment, and she stopped thinking about it almost as soon as she started. She curled up in a ball inside the tiny tent, Mutt huddled close beside her, and waited it out.

The silence jerked her awake. It took a moment to orient herself, to accustom herself to the quiet. Incredibly, she must have dozed. She raised her head and met Mutt's alert yellow eyes. The dog gave a soft, questioning whine. Kate raised her head, neck stiff, shoulders tense. The length of the sleeping bag, the pack, the inside of the tent, all were covered with a layer of fine, crystalline snow. She kicked her sleeping bag clear, unzipped it, then the tent flap. Crawling outside, she rose to her feet on legs that trembled a little.

Everywhere she looked the features of the Quilaks had changed, and changed radically. The southeast face of Mount Kanuyaq had been swept clean of snow and ice, scoured down to bare rock. The mouth of Sisik Glacier was filled from wall to wall with a flow of snow that reached out a mile and a half into the Valley of Death.

The only way Kate recognized the Barnes Wall, a five thousand-foot drop from Angqaq Peak to Sleighter Glacier, was by its location. Every feature, every fissure on it had been altered, shifted, broken. Carlson Icefall's once tiered, stairstep surface had been polished smooth by a gigantic hand and now gleamed in the twilight like a marble flagstone.

The Valley of Death itself had been ripped open in every direction. There wasn't a cornice left intact on top of a glacier wall as far as the eye could see. Everywhere, the fresh blue of newly exposed glacier ice gleamed coldly in the setting sun's refracted glow.

As Kate watched, the sun slipped behind the Alaska Range, leaving only a band of misty mauve on the western horizon. One after another, stars found their way through the firmament to appear overhead. The air itself seemed to glitter with a thousand diamonds, the glint of starlight off spindrift. The mountains stood still and serene.

It was beauty. It was innocence. It was peace.

It was a lie. Kate turned her back on it, repacked the tent and went in search.

But there was no sign of Lottie. There was no sign of Lottie's rifle. There was no sign of Lottie's pack, or of Lottie's tent, or of any of the rest of her gear. There was no sign of Lottie's tracks.

There should have been something—a mitten, a boot, a half-empty bag of trail mix. Kate raised her head from contemplation of the bland stretch of snow at her feet and stared up the long valley, her eyes narrowed, trying to see through the deepening twilight, around the jumbled remains of the avalance.

There was nothing, no movement, only the calm after the storm. Kate shoved her hands in her pockets and cocked an eye at Mutt. "For that matter, there was no sign of our tracks, either. That tidal wave of frozen water pretty much obliterated everything that got in its way."

Mutt, sitting with her tail curled around her paws, looked the picture of patience as she waited for Kate to give her the signal to start tracking.

"Well?" Kate asked her. "Who's to say Big Bump didn't eat her alive? It could have been us. It damn near was us. Why not Lottie?"

The more she thought about it, the better it sounded. Resettling the pack on her shoulders, she turned and began retracing her steps in the direction of the base camp. Surprised but pleased to be going in a direction of declining altitude, Mutt rose to her feet and followed.

As always, the journey down seemed half as long as the journey up. The Koreans were alive, which surprised Kate, and touchingly glad to see her, which did not. Their radio, recovered from the bottom of a brand-new twelve-foot ravine not three feet from the front of their tent, was crusted with ice and battered from the fall. She switched it on without much hope and rejoiced when by a minor miracle it came to life. The volume knob was turned all the way to the right and Dan O'Brian's voice blared out over the still arctic night.

"Kanuyuq Base, Kanuyuq Base, this is Ranger 1, Ranger 1, come in. Goddammit, you guys! Where the hell are you! Answer up! Say something, even if it's in Korean!"

The Koreans cried out at the sound of his voice and fell sobbing into each other's arms. Kate lunged for the volume knob and turned it down. Keying the mike, she said, "Danny boy, you got yourself a mouth on you could wake up a wooly mammoth."

A brief silence. "Kate? Kate, is that you?"

"That's me. I'm about five thousand feet above your base camp, around the southern mouth of what used to be the Valley of Death. George's two Koreans are here, too, and they're okay."

"Never mind them, what about you?"

"I'm fine. We just have an earthquake?"

"No shit we just had an earthquake, about six-point-two's worth on the Richter scale. For a while there I thought the whole Park was going to slide into the Gulf of Alaska. I'll never make fun of your '64 quake stories again, Kate. What's the mountain look like?"

Kate gave a short laugh and settled for "You won't believe it."

Even over the radio's static she could hear the change in his voice. "What's the base camp look like?"

Kate, having already sighted in on where the base camp used to be with Bobby's set of Bushnell field glasses, replied, "What base camp?"

Valuable airtime was wasted with a string of words for which the using of over the public airwaves the FCC fines heavily. Kate stood it patiently for as long as she was able, but she was tired and hungry and her patience didn't last long.

She clicked the transmitter key, interrupting the circuit, until he shut up. "Fire up the Llama and come get these two nitwits before I shove them into a crevasse."

ten

THE Lama showed up less than an hour later and took on the Koreans. Behind them Kate shoved in as much of their gear as had been salvaged and stood back. Dan looked around. "Come on, Kate, quit screwing around! Get aboard!"

"Go!" she yelled over the sound of the engine.

"Quit screwing around!"

"Go on!" she yelled. "I'm heading up to the summit! I've never been!"

Dan doffed the headset and slipped out of the chopper. He ducked around to stand next to her. "What's the matter with you?"

"I've never been to the summit," Kate repeated.

He looked at her, one eyebrow raised. "You're the last person I ever expected to get summit fever."

"The climbers always want to do the last leg on their own. The weather's good. There'll never be a better day to see what all the shouting's about. Plus, I can take a look at what the quake did to the route."

He squinted up the valley. "Can you do ten thousand feet in a day?"

"It's only five thousand up."

"And five thousand back," he pointed out, "and you know as well as I do coming down's always more dangerous than going up."

She shrugged and spread her hands. He swore at her.

"You gonna keep on after Lottie, is that what this is about?"

"Lottie's dead," she said flatly.

He gave her a sharp look. "Lottie's better at wilderness survival than just about anyone I know, including you. You find her body?"

"Nope." Kate shook her head. "But she's dead. Avalanche got her. Buried her without a trace."

He looked from Kate's expressionless face to the pass below the East Buttress of Angqaq Peak and back again. "How tidy."

"I thought so."

"No point in looking for the body, I guess."

"No point at all," Kate agreed.

"But you want to go mountain climbing anyway."

"Yup."

He threw up his hands. "Okay, fine, all right. Weather's about near perfect, forecast is for more of the same. Take the radio with you, and call me from Carlson Icefall. I'll pick you up there."

"Okay. See you tomorrow noon at the latest?"

He drew himself up, affronted. "You hitting the Park Service up for a totally unauthorized ride in a department vehicle?"

"Yes."

He grinned. "You got it. See you then. You coming?" he yelled at Mutt.

Mutt looked longingly at the helicopter, pleadingly up at Kate, and barked a resigned negative. Dan shrugged. "You're both nuts. See you later."

She labored up the slope, panting in the oxygen-thin air. She climbed ten steps in the powdery, shifting snow, rested ten, climbed ten, rested ten. Mutt walked when she did, stopped when she did. It was the first time Kate had ever seen Mutt look even remotely tired.

Every thousand feet or so she forced food and water

down both of them, marveling all the while at their luck. Angqaq Peak was not a technically difficult climb, so long as you stuck to the route up Nicolo Glacier, between Carlson Icefall and the East Buttress. But it was high and the air was thin and the weather was usually for shit, with winds that had broken a 110-mph anemometer just a month before, and temperatures that combined with those winds to result in chill factors routinely registering at minus 100 degrees Fahrenheit and lower.

But not that night. That night was a night out of a fairy tale. A full moon had risen two hours after sundown, and moonlight reflected off the snow and ice, lighting the landscape so that it was almost impossible for the two climbers to stumble or lose their way. There wasn't a hint of wind, and where the light of the moon did not obliterate them, stars shone like holes burnt into the fabric of the night. It was cold, clear and absolutely still, and the journey up was turning into more of a hike than a climb.

A continuous ripple of rock, rifts of ice and high folds of drifted snow had hidden the summit from them almost all the way up, which was why when they attained it Kate had almost started down the other side before she realized it. She halted, breathing hard, one mittened hand on Mutt's head.

They stood together at the top of the world—Miklluni Peak on their right, Mount Kanuyaq on their left, the Child at their feet, the rest of the jagged summits gathered at a respectful distance before Angqaq's proud and disdainful zenith. Challenging from below, from above the mountains seemed almost deferential. Kate looked from them to the moon and the stars hanging far above, and for the first time, she understood the true allure of mountain climbing.

There was elation, there was triumph, there was pride in achieving the summit, yes, but most of all there was a shift in perspective. From below, the view was of the

mountains and the heavens, equally unattainable. From here, it was the mountains below and the heavens above and herself in between, herself, an insignificant, puny little mortal between immortals. A glint caught the corner of her eye, and she turned her head quickly, to catch the last glimpse of a meteor streaking across the sky in a thin smear of astral dust. The heavens were alive, too, as alive as the earth below. So Frost was right after all, she thought. The best thing we're put here for's to see.

Another part of her protested, Is that all? Not to do? Only to see?

"It's enough," she said out loud. "More than enough. If your eyes are open it's a full-time job."

Slender tendrils of feathered aurora felt their way down from the north, shedding their cold glow over the broken arctic landscape, ephemeral ribbons of confectioner's sugar spun into pastel strands of pale green and red and blue and white. Closer they crept, and closer, until they were directly overhead and Kate could hear them talking among themselves, a muted, electric hum of gossipy comment over the broken scene below.

Instinctively, Kate fumbled beneath her parka and around her waist. The old Eskimos thought that the Northern Lights reached down and snatched people away, but that you could protect yourself against them with your knife. It was one of Ekaterina's favorite stories, and she had told it over and over and over again to the small granddaughter perched on her knee. It was only a story; still, the hilt of the knife felt solid and comforting in Kate's hand. She looked up again, marveling in the light and color, at the sound. After a while those sounds began to work together, to take on a rhythm, and without conscious thought Kate began to move with them. She half crouched over legs bent at the knees and her feet stamped lightly against the hard-packed snow, in time with the aurora.

A red band arced down and she lunged forward to meet

it, daring it to snatch her up. A tendril of green shifted and swirled above her, and she flung up a hand and sketched her homage against it. One white finger tickled the surface of the snow at her feet, and she danced with it, step for step. Agudar, master spirit, keeper of the game, loomed white and round far above and shed a steady glow over them all, and in the light of that steady glow the spirits of the dead gathered round to bear witness, but Lottie was not among them. Lighthearted, joyous, Kate matched steps with a band of red that swirled and wrapped back upon itself above her head.

The light increased in the east, and the aurora slipped away in search of other dancing partners. Kate's feet slowed, and stopped, her breath coming hard in the thin air. Mutt came to stand next to her, and together they faced into the rising sun, watching as the pale gold of morning slipped over the knife-edged peaks, spilled into the valleys, sparked against the distant blue of Prince William Sound. The sky bleached from dark to light, and the first seeking rays of sunlight felt their way over the horizon to crown the new day with cold fire.

And the sun rose full up into the sky, and the night fled into the west and all magic with it, and Kate was abandoned at the top of a white world stripped clean and polished by the clear, honest, merciless light of morning. She felt stripped and polished herself, refined down to her essential elements. It was as if she had been roused from a long sleep filled with dreams to satiate desires both subtle and gross, only to be greeted by a new world with more promise than any dream. Or perhaps it was only that she looked at it through new eyes.

She smiled at this unaccustomed flight of fancy. "I do believe romance is getting the better of me this morning," she told Mutt. "Sorry about that."

Mutt's expression indicated that, romance notwithstanding, they had pressed their luck far enough and it was more than time to get the hell off Big Bump

and back to where a reasonable person, four-footed or otherwise, might expect to find food and shelter when a storm blew up unexpectedly, as storms were prone to do, and especially here.

Mutt was right. Kate took a last, pensive look down the eastern sweep of the Quilaks, appreciating as never before how vast was the interior of the North American continent, and how high nineteen thousand feet was. A thought occurred that made her groan beneath her breath. "You know what this means, don't you?" she told Mutt.

Mutt looked puzzled, and Kate said sadly, "God help us, it looks like Middle Finger for two, babe."

She shrugged into her pack and, Mutt at her side, began the long trek down.